MW01036732

BEAUTY AND THE BOSS

Book 1 in the Billionaire's Obsession Series

R. S. ELLIOT

© Copyright 2019 by AmazingLifeForever

All rights reserved.

It is not legal to reproduce, duplicate, or transmit any part of this document in either electronic means or in printed format. Recording of this publication is strictly prohibited and any storage of this document is not allowed unless with written permission from the publisher except for the use of brief quotations in a book review.

This book is a work of fiction. Any resemblance to persons, living or dead, or places, events or locations is purely coincidental.

❀ Created with Vellum

AUTHOR'S NOTE

Welcome to my world of sexy, contemporary romance where you will find Billionaires, Alpha heroes, Bad boys and some extra naughtiness! If you are looking for something sweet, sexy and with a happily ever after, then look no further!

Beauty and the BOSS is Book 1 in my Billionaire's Obsession Series which comprises of 5 Hot and Steamy Full Length Romance Novels.

Each individual book in this series will be a standalone and offer an HEA and can be read in any order but I would strongly propose to read the prequel first and then follow the reading sequence from Book1 to Book 5 in the series.

Grab the FREE Prequel to Beauty and the BOSS at the following link: https://dl.bookfunnel.com/sdttkzrxl9

Join my Exclusive Reader Group where I announce Giveaways and Release dates https://www.facebook.com/groups/851309431881791/

Like my Facebook page to get updates, fun, and prizes!
https://www.facebook.com/AuthorRSElliot

Join me on Instagram -
   https://www.instagram.com/rselliotauthor/

If you wish to get in contact, please email me at rselliot@amaz-inglifeforever.com

instagram.com/rselliotauthor

Chapter One

LUKE

I arrived at Vernon's party a half hour late. Late enough to show I didn't want to be there, but not late enough to get on my sister's bad side. The space they rented on the top floor of a premier New York hotel encased in glass, offered a view of the skyline that would have been breathtaking if my own view at home didn't rival it.

As with all Vernon parties, the cream of the city's business class was here: high rolling investors mingled with heiress debutantes, and families who made their fortunes in mutual funds or startup schemes shook hands with each other politely. The Vernons were old money, but they stayed in the game through their sizable investment portfolio and charitable giving. This small bites and champagne hour was in honor of their youngest son, Eric, who recently found moderate success in some business venture or other. In my mind, his success was entirely unremarkable, because the greatest windfall that had ever happened to him was his marriage to my sister, Sarah.

"Luke!" Sarah said when she saw me. She was hanging on Eric's arm, thronged by a group of men in suits who were having a somber conversation about something, probably money. A glass of champagne bubbled in her hand, and she radiated a rosy glow that her dress matched. She was thrilled for her husband, so I could at least pretend to get along with him for an hour. For Sarah, if for no one else.

I crossed the room to my sister and brother-in-law, ignoring the heads that turned when I did. A novelty for the first year or two of SkyBlue's success, I got used to the glances I got when I was out. Those who didn't recognize me saw a man in a suit that cost more than a month's wages. Those who did probably knew my reputation as one of the youngest and richest C-suite executives in the city, valued in the hundred millions. Some of them had probably seen the write-ups in Forbes, GQ, or Popular Science. I tried to keep a low profile, but when you dared to be wealthy, young, and the face of a company that manufactured controversial self-driving cars, the press were hard to shake. People stared.

"Sarah," I said warmly, and kissed my sister on the cheek, light enough to not disturb her makeup or get any of it on my suit jacket. I came straight from the office and was wearing the same Tom Ford number that had seen me through a hectic ten hours of work.

"I'm so happy you came!" She crooned, and she *did* look happy. I gave her a smile that probably looked closer to a grimace. According to my little sister, I should make more of a concerted effort to socialize in my off hours, or at least allow myself to have off hours in the first place. This gesture of good faith was the first attempt I made to take her advice in several months.

"Of course, I came."

I turned my attention to her husband, and the smile became harder to hold.

"Eric," I said, and extended my hand stiffly.

Eric Vernon gave it a weak shake, a courteous smile flickering across his face before he turned back to his inane conversation about cryptocurrency with the other men around him. I always considered Eric a bit boring and had of course been prepared to hate him when Sarah told me she fell in love with someone who swept her off her feet and proposed within a matter of months. He had seemed reckless to me at the time, and I didn't want any man wrecking the life Sarah worked so hard to build for herself.

It turned out that he was an acceptable, even diligent husband, but a terrible business partner. He had offered to invest money in SkyBlue when the company was still in its infancy when he was still attempting to get on my good side, and I had foolishly taken him at his word.

The money had never shown up.

"I'm going to get a drink," I said crisply.

Sarah opened her mouth to say something, maybe to insist that I stay and socialize, but then Eric's arm wrapped around her waist, one of the other men said something that made her laugh, and I made a break for it. I slipped through the sea of shined shoes and glimmering dresses to the discreet white table that had been set up along the back wall. It was indicative of this kind of function: three types of wine, crackers with elaborate spreads and dressings, and fruit tartlets for dessert. Everything was of course, impeccably made and shipped in from one of the best Italian restaurants in the city. I popped a few rosemary crostini topped with whipped chevre and caviar into my mouth (it would have to suffice for dinner since I hadn't ordered anything into the office) and poured myself a half glass of the driest champagne I could find.

"How can you drink that stuff?" A woman's voice, dulcet with flirtation, said behind me. "Wouldn't you like something a little sweeter?"

I closed my eyes and swallowed a groan. Whoever it was, I didn't need it tonight. It was probably some diplomat, or socialite, or investment banker who would make eyes at me for a half an hour hoping for a one-night stand or a sugar daddy. I was too tired.

I turned around, trying to keep my expression neutral. Claire, Eric's youngest sister, was gazing at me from under her lashes, running her finger coyly around the rim of her champagne glass. The last time I had seen Claire was at my sister's wedding when she was an awkward overgrown teen in an ill-fitting bridesmaid dress. Now, she had lost some of her baby fat and filled out in womanly curves. Her bedazzled kelly green dress flaunted it with a plunging neckline, but I wasn't sure she was old enough to drink the fizzing mimosa in her hand.

Claire was, unequivocally, the last thing I needed tonight.

"I prefer a balanced drink," I said, throwing back half my champagne in one swallow. "Too much sugar gets overpowering. You lose the individual notes."

"Oh, sure," Claire said sagely, as though she was a regular sommelier in training. She wasn't an unattractive girl and had piled her long chestnut hair up on top of her head in a messy, sexy half-done way. Her high cheekbones caught the light and gleamed with a golden shimmer, and her breasts were... very present. I allowed myself an indulgent glance before reminding myself that she was Eric's sister and needed no more encouragement.

4

Claire glanced appraisingly into her glass. "Mimosas are nice, but I prefer cocktails. Bacardi, Maker's Mark, that kind of thing. You know what they say." Her eyes sparkled at me, devilishly. She was going to make some poor man very happy with that chaotic sexual energy, but I didn't want to play with her kind of fire. "Liquor is quicker."

"That's true," I said weakly, and silently berated myself for not following my usual routine of politely turning down my sister's invitations, sending a have fun without me text, and then going home to read emails and press releases before falling asleep sometime around two in the morning. It wasn't exactly fun, but it was a well-worn path to stability and success that I could trust, and it didn't have any Claires on it.

"So, what notes can you pick up?" She asked, nodded to my glass. "In that."

I sighed. I was in no mood to give a tasting lesson, and I wasn't very good at it, to start.

"Oh, I don't know, apples, pear? The usual white fruits. Maybe something floral." I took another sip, pulling the wine through my teeth. "Lavender? I could be wrong."

"That's so cool. Could you teach me how to do that? I'm a quick study, and I'm good with my tongue."

She was staring me down with those impish eyes, wanting to make sure the implication hit home. There was no getting rid of her. Just as I was debating telling her to find some other guy to harass, I was hit in the legs by a tiny body moving at immense speed.

"Uncle Luke!" My nephew Ryan shrieked in delight. His reddish hair was askew, the tail of his dress shirt had been yanked out of his slacks, and he had a smear of something that looked like strawberry sauce on his face. Obviously, he had been having a better night than me.

I had never been happier to see my seven-year-old nephew.

I discarded my champagne glass and bent down to sweep him into my arms, hoisting him up onto my hip with a grin. He was light for his size, and I was a sucker for picking him up whenever he asked or when he got tired. When Sarah and I took him to see Aladdin on Broadway, he had complained that his feet were tired while we were standing in line, and I carried him, like a big sap, for the rest of the night. That was to say nothing of the souvenirs and root beer float I bought him on our way home. Sarah told me I was going to spoil him, but I didn't care. What was the point of having all this money if I didn't spend it on Ryan, and the other people I cared about? My parents had never been able to do that for Sarah and I. I wanted Ryan to know how cherished he was.

"Look at you!" I said, forgetting about Claire entirely. "You've gotten huge!"

Ryan squealed with laughter as I hoisted him up onto my shoulders, clinging to the model car he had been toting around like a security blanket. He had been nonverbal the first three years of his life and was still a shy kid despite becoming an avid talker in his first-grade class. He always carried some little toy around with him to make him feel safe. He was into vehicles right now; it had been dinosaur shaped sponges last week.

"What car is this?" I asked.

"It's a Corvette!" Ryan explained and made an engine noise with his lips.

"A classic, nice choice. A bit flashy for me, but I'm a boring old man."

Ryan found this self-depreciation so funny he burst into laughter again, and I couldn't help but smile. Ryan was my favorite relief from the world of boardrooms and press meetings. He was brighter by a mile than I was at that age and was always inventing contraptions with Legos or trying to take apart his mother's cell phone to figure out how it worked. It had been that demand of knowledge and his determination to get it. I considered it my mission to make sure Ryan always had the support he needed to cultivate those interests and become something great.

"Ryan, I was talking to Uncle Luke," Claire said, sounding all the more miffed for the thick layer of false sweetness she slathered on to her words. "Why don't you go find mommy and let the grown-ups talk about grown-up things."

"He's fine, Claire," I said, adding internally *and the two of us have nothing to talk about.*

Claire chewed on her lip in irritation but didn't say anything else. Instead, she fixed herself another mimosa and slithered away into the crowd, defeated. Something told me I wouldn't be seeing the last of her, but for now, I was grateful for the reprieve.

"Can we go to the pool?" Ryan asked, running his toy car along the highway of my shoulder.

"The pool? Buddy, it's dark outside. We're in our nice clothes. We can't go swimming right now."

"No, not swimming! I just want to look at it."

"You just want to go stare at a pool? While there's this whole party going on right here?"

"Pleeeeeeeease?"

"Alright, alright! You win."

Ryan hooted in triumph as I moved towards one of the sleek

glass doors that led out to the sizable rooftop pool included with this premiere event suite. Multicolored lights pulsated gently beneath the water, reflecting off dark lacquered tiles giving the whole deck an elegant feel. The noises of the city drifted up from the pavement below; honking horns, shouts of laughter, screeching tires, and a distant drum line rhythm. When they said New York never slept, it was true, and I knew we were in the throes of the late-night rush of bodies from bars to restaurants to clubs to music venues.

"There it is," I said, pulling my nephew off my shoulders and setting him upright on the ground. "Go hog-wild. But don't get your clothes wet, or your mother will kill me."

Despite being high-spirited and sometimes stubborn, Ryan was fairly well-behaved and placed himself near the edge of the shallow end of the pool where he could watch the lights beneath the water change color. He ran his car along the edge of the pool's tile, sometimes gently dipping its wheels in the water and glancing up at me to see if this was forbidden or not. I let him have it.

"Daddy is from Chicago," He said, with the grave, wise air of a child who had just learned a new fact. "And mommy is from Queens."

"That's right, good job."

"Chicago is in Illinois."

"Yes, it is."

"Are you from Illinois, Uncle Luke?"

"No, I'm from Queens, too, kiddo. I grew up in the same house as your mommy. She's my sister, remember? Your mommy is my sister, which makes you my nephew."

We had gone over all this before, back when his class had

been studying family trees. Ryan had been thrilled to connect all the little paper leaves he cut out and scrawled our names on to stick to his tree. They must have moved on to geography now, by the sound of it.

"Did you and mommy live in a house when you were kids?"

I thought back to the cramped, squat roundhouse we shared with three other families. It faced the streets where children played in open fire hydrants one day and ducked behind cars to avoid drive-by shootings the next. Ryan had never even been to a neighborhood like that before; he probably couldn't even wrap his tiny brain around what the experience of poverty was like, not even around something as simple as not having his room all to himself.

"We did, but we shared it with some other kids as well."

"Your friends?"

"Some of them, yeah."

I thought of Nico, gap-toothed and smiling with his olive complexion that tanned deeply in the summer, and of Marcus, bookish but spunky and always smelling of the shea butter his mother worked into his tight coils of black hair. I also thought of the bigger boys, with their shit talk and split lips, who liked to hang around our stoop smoking cigarettes and swapping tall tales. As I got older, they became insistent I start rolling around with the gang they had joined, for my own protection, they insisted, and so I could learn how to be a man. Marcus and I always refused, dealing with their slurs and put-downs, but they almost got Nico. He got spooked the first time he saw someone get shot and showed up back on his mother's porch rattled and tear-streaked. We had all stayed out of it after that, and Nico and Marcus had grown into men I was still proud to call my friends.

"Some of them weren't so nice, though. They liked to fight."

"Mommy says I'm not allowed to hit."

"That's right; we don't hit."

"Have you ever been in a fight?"

"A couple of times, when I was younger."

Ryan seemed delighted and scandalized by this in equal measure. What he didn't need to know was that I developed a reputation as a scrapper in my middle school years, throwing punches at guys way out of my weight class. I was so angry; at my father, for being so absent, and at my teachers, for not believing that any of the kids from my neighborhood were worth anything. Mad at the whole damn system that kept my family trapped in a cycle of debt and scarcity. The only one who could talk sense into me when I started seeing red and itching for a fight was Martha. Aunt Martha, to be specific, though we weren't related. She was a middle-aged woman who lived across the street from me and had raised two children of her own while also, somehow always looking out for the neighborhood punks.

She would sit with me on her front stoop while I iced a black eye and feed me her homemade tamales, telling me that I had more choices than I thought I did. I had the choice to keep getting black eyes, keep failing my classes, and let the way my father spoke to me determine my self-worth. Or I could choose to walk away from losing battles, to cultivate all that intelligence my teachers loved to say I was squandering and to focus on my shit while my father figured out his.

Aunt Maratha, I truly believe, saved my life.

After I got into MIT, she floated my first semester of expenses out of her retirement savings to ensure that I could stay enrolled long enough to find scholarships. She always believed that if I were put in the right environment with the right people, I would soar, and MIT proved her right. Within three years, I had assembled a crack team of software designers, engineers, investors, and technicians and had launched SkyBlue Solutions, one of the first tech companies dedicated exclusively to autonomous car technology. By the time the company went public after the release of our first ever model, a car featuring assisted driving technology and the ability to switch to automatic driving in case of an emergency, I was worth more money than anyone in our neighborhood ever dreamed of. One of the first things I did after I got my cut of the sales was to retire Aunt Martha permanently, with trust funds set up for each of her children and grandchildren.

"Can I go to your old house?" Ryan asked, getting bolder as he dipped his whole car into the water, submerging his hands in the process.

"No, I don't think so."

"Why?"

"Because it's not a very special place. I don't think you'd like it."

Sarah appeared through one of the glass doors behind us, throwing her eyes around for her son.

"There you are!" She said. Then, as she saw her son's proximity to the pool, she added, "Really, Luke."

"I'm watching him; there's nothing to worry about."

"Nothing to worry about!" Ryan echoed. Sarah smiled at him despite herself. Her pale blonde hair had been cut into a sleek bob recently, probably to save on time and maintenance as motherhood caught up with her.

"Well, boys, we're about to have some cake, so head back inside."

That was the only push Ryan needed. He scrambled to his

feet and tore off in the direction of cake at top speed. Sarah laid her hand on my arm and walked me at a meandering pace back into the party.

"It does really mean a lot to me that you came. Are you having fun?"

"As much fun as I ever have at these things."

Her brows furrowed slightly.

"I know they're not your favorite. But I think it's good to think about something other than the company sometimes."

"There's just so much to be done, Sarah."

The last five years had been a whirlwind of sleepless nights, hectic press conferences, and insane paydays. But my work was finally paying off, and as SkyBlue entered its third production season with all new offerings in both luxury and economy models, I was feeling confident that we were here to stay. Only two other companies in the world were doing what we were doing, and their technology was by no means as well integrated as ours. But they were still outperforming us due to charitable donations from philanthropists looking to prevent accidents and save the planet in the process. We were doubling down on our eco-friendly features to meet the demand. I wouldn't be satisfied until I knew I was the best. Until I was positive that SkyBlue products stood at the top of the heap no matter the test conditions.

My sister smiled at me.

"That might be true, but I know Ryan is happy you were able to come, anyway."

The noise and bustle of the party was fast approaching, and I could see Ryan bobbing excitedly around a caterer ferrying the artisan cake to a table in the center of the room.

"At that rate, thank you for inviting me."

Sarah gave my arm a loving squeeze.

"I'm going to make a social animal out of you yet, Luke. Just you wait."

I smirked down at her.

"You can try."

Chapter Two

EMILY

$\mathcal{I}$ tugged a brush through my long, snarled red hair as my phone alarm alerted me that if I didn't hurry, I would be late for my first day of work at SkyBlue. I silenced the alarm with a jab of my finger, then abandoned making my waist-length hair cooperate and instead swirled it up into a quick but passable bun. If I wanted breakfast, I would have to skimp on makeup. A few passes of mascara and a smudge of blush were enough to bring life to my face.

The phone started buzzing again, but this time to signal an incoming call. I made an irritated huff and reached out to silence it, then realized it was my mother calling. I put her call through on speaker mode and answered while I stabbed bobby pins into my hair.

"Hi Mom."

"Emily! How are you, sweetie?"

"I'm good. Getting ready for work."

"I'm so proud of you for landing this internship. You're going to do so well."

"Thanks, Mom," I said, smiling even though I didn't strictly believe her. I still wasn't entirely sure how I, as a last-minute applicant and photography major, had landed a summer internship at one of the top tech companies in New York, but I had always been told my interviewing skills were excellent. When I wanted something, I was my own best advocate, and I had *wanted* that internship. Well, not exactly. The internship was irrelevant. What I truly wanted was to perform well enough to get the letter of recommendation I needed to apply for the summer study experience in Paris next year. I came within a hair's breadth of being accepted into the program all expenses paid this year but was denied because of my lack of work experience.

"How are you feeling, Bunny?" She asked, using her childhood nickname for me. There was a distant noise in the background, the shuffling of items, and the chatter of voices. She was probably calling me from the front desk of the hotel where she worked as a concierge.

"Alright, I think. Nervous."

"Of course you're nervous! It's natural. How did you sleep last night?"

"Uh..." I glanced over at my narrow twin bed, sheets disheveled from a fitful night of nightmares and cold sweats. The jangling daytime nerves and startling at any loud sound had improved over the last few weeks, but I was still having trouble getting any decent sleep. "Alright. I got enough shut-eye."

"Nightmares again?"

"It's alright," I insisted. "Nothing serious."

"Emily, someone held you at gunpoint. It's alright if you're still shaken up."

I saw my mouth form a thin red line in the mirror as I brushed some pomade onto my thick brows. I had tried to drop hints whenever I spoke to my mother (and she had been calling an awful lot lately) that I didn't want to talk about the carjacking. It was bad enough that I kept dreaming about that night, about being dragged from my idling car at a stoplight and thrown to the ground while a masked man screamed threats at me. I had never been so terrified in my entire life, and I really thought for a moment that he was going to shoot me dead on the concrete. It was only luck that had saved my life: luck, and a mysterious stranger on a motorcycle.

The man had appeared out of nowhere at the end of the street on a purring matte black bike and scared off the carjackers. When they escaped with my car, the man had pulled me up off the ground and spoke to me kindly in a rich voice, doing his best to calm me down. He even offered to give me a ride home. That was my first time on a motorcycle, and we rocketed down the streets of Queens with my arms latched tightly around his leather jacket-clad chest. I never saw his face, since he never took off his sleek black helmet, but I remembered his eyes, vibrant green with almost invisible smile lines at the corners.

If I was honest with myself, I had become a little... fixated. I had intrusive thoughts about the rider as often as I thought of the carjacking, albeit much warmer thoughts. I spent an embarrassing amount of my time swinging from terror and shame I couldn't shake to dreamy idolizations of my rescuer. Who was he? Did he live in the city? What did he do for a living? Was he married? And of course, above all else: was I ever going to see him again?

Those kinds of thoughts couldn't be normal. I had heard of victims of trauma sexually fixating on elements of their trauma to self-soothe and infuse bad memories with a little good. Maybe this guy had just been in the right place at the right time to bear the brunt of my coping mechanism. Or maybe, there was something more to our meeting. Maybe there was something like the hand of God in it or fate.

"Emily?" My mother asked again, bringing me back to myself.

"Oh, sorry! Yes, Mom, I'm fine. Really. I'm getting over it, I promise."

"Well, that's good to hear. Listen, your sister and I have been talking, and we think it's important for you to get another car..."

Panic did a tapdance in my stomach.

"What? No, that's totally unnecessary. This is New York, no one owns a car, anyway. And why does Darlene get an opinion?"

"But you're all the way out there in Queens! How will you visit home?"

"I'll take the train."

"Bunny, come on. Let me do this for you, please."

I took a deep breath, gathering up my purse and phone charger.

"I'm not going to say no if you want to get me another car, but I can't promise I'll get around to using it."

My mother laughed on the other end, then pressed the phone to her breast as she turned to tell someone that the fourth floor needed more towels. I swallowed dryly while I waited for her to return. There was a hot flush in my cheeks and the back of my neck as I tried to remember how to breathe. The panic was coming back, clawing its way up my throat. I couldn't bring myself to tell my mother that I hadn't been able to get behind the wheel of a car for three weeks after the carjacking. I almost passed out from hot-faced shallow-breathing dizziness the one time I rode the bus after the incident. I had been sticking to the metro exclusively because there was something about the gentle rocking of the subway train in the dark embrace of the underground tunnels that was different enough from a car to comfort me.

I had no idea when I was going to be able to shake the after-effects of my trauma, but I didn't want to involve my mother in my struggles. She had been working so hard since my father died a few years ago to be strong for a thirteen-year-old Darlene and for me. She didn't need another crisis on her plate.

"I've just had a large group come in," my mother said. "But I'll call this weekend, and we can talk it through, alright? I'm sure we can find some little used car that will be perfect for you."

"Sounds good," I said weakly.

"And have the best first day of work. I know you're going to be great."

I smiled at this. My mother wasn't always the best at reading other people, certainly not her children, but she was as genuine and giving as ever.

I tried not to worry that she was being too generous, and might land herself right back in debt after she spent years clawing out of it. Something they never tell you about unex-pected deaths is that they're expensive. When my father dropped dead of an aneurysm at fifty, my family had no game plan. We had no idea how we would pay our bills without his income, or which of his debts would be canceled or assigned to my mother, or where we would come up with the money for even the most basic funeral. My father had always been in charge of finances in our family, and when he died, my mother found herself unprepared for the avalanche of paperwork and debt collection calls. It had been a dark time, especially when we were coping with grief at the same time.

Darlene started acting out, mom threw herself into her work, insisting that everything was fine and me, well... I drifted. My father had been my rock my whole life, my confidant, counselor, and comforter. Without his strong, nurturing, presence in my life, I felt like part of my identity had been stripped away. It didn't help that I was sixteen, and already utterly unsure of myself.

"And you're sure you don't want to come home for a little while?" My mother asked. The jostling voices talking over each other in the background were louder now, and I knew we only had seconds before she had to hang up.

"I'm sure, Mom. I want to stay here while I get settled at my job. But I'll visit soon, I promise."

"Okay, Bunny. Love you so much."

"Love you too. Bye."

I sighed as I hung up, then turned back to my mirror and continued applying blush to my ashen cheeks as though that could make up for how sapped I felt. I loved my mother, but she could be draining, and I still wasn't comfortable thinking unexpectedly about my father's death.

Without my father, applying for college, looking for jobs, even getting out of bed in the morning to go to school started to feel insurmountable. It was only by drawing on the love of my friends and reserves of strength that I didn't know I had that I could move out and start my studies last year at NYU. Going home would be moving backward in my personal development. And it would likely be an even bigger emotional and financial burden on my mother. She had her hands full trying to be a single parent to Darlene in the small New Jersey split level they shared. Darlene wasn't all bad, as much as she would like people to think. I was positive she would pull through her rebellious streak, but the smoking and the angry music sent my mother into a tizzy. I knew that coming home would only exacerbate things since Darlene and I currently got along best when we communicated through memes shared on Facebook and intermittent phone calls, not face-to-face.

No, New York was my responsibility. I chose it; the noise, the high rent, the crime rates, and the glaring lack of square footage in every available space. But I would be lying if I said I didn't love it. I found the hustle and bustle energizing, and there were so many beautiful landmarks and interesting new people to photograph in a city so diverse and storied. Nothing compared to my beloved Paris, which I'd dreamed about visiting since I was eight years old, but for now, New York would do.

The subway ride to SkyBlue was uneventful, but I spent most of it with my stomach in knots. I was full of first day jitters, especially with a company as huge and well-known as this tech magnate. It didn't help that I knew next to nothing about cars or software design, but I guess I didn't have to as an administrative intern who assisted with data entry. At least, that's what they had told me at my brief orientation two weeks prior. I was swept along too fast to get my bearings through a few rooms of glass, then seated at a table and made to sign about a hundred contracts and nondisclosure agreements. Then I was moved on to a lecture about professional dress. It was more like a very stressful HR meeting than an orientation.

When I stepped out of the subway entrance and onto the busy concrete slab across the street from SkyBlue, my heart was in my shoes. The building was massive, a monstrosity of steel and glass stretching up into a needle-thin point in the sky. It flaunted its modernity, lording it over other nearby buildings with their stone gargoyles or seventies ergonomic designs. I felt dwarfed by it, and I wasn't even close enough to be swallowed up by the steady stream of men in tailored suits and women clutching designer handbags rushing from the entrance.

I swallowed hard, glanced down at the room number and name scrawled into my day planner, and reminded myself to think of Paris. Then I crossed the street.

I only got turned around twice looking for the floor I would work on and the woman I was scheduled to meet upon arriving: Sonia Somers. She was seated on the edge of one of the wide desks that filled the open-plan office when I arrived. She smiled brightly at me with lips painted the color of plums. Her suit jacket was mauve, and she wore fashionable wide-legged slacks and delicate gold jewelry that looked, to my untrained eye, very expensive. I hadn't realized people in the tech world were so high fashion, but I guess I should have known better. This was New York, after all.

"Sonia?" I asked, extending my hand for a firm handshake. I had learned to do that from my father, who was a born salesman.

"That's right! You must be Emily,"

"That's right," I said and felt a little awkward standing there in my plain black flats and my fast fashion skirt and blouse clutching a scuffed handbag I picked up from target. Sonia's handbag was a sleek black velvet number on a golden chain, and a logo I couldn't recognize but knew was designer. I didn't think it was a knockoff.

"I'm so happy to finally meet you. HR and the hiring committee had great things to say. As you probably know, this isn't an easy gig to land."

"I had a suspicion. Thank you for saying so."

"I'll be your transition supervisor for your first few months here. I work closely with all the new hires and interns in this department to make sure everything goes smoothly for them and to answer any questions they have. You won't be with us long enough to be transferred to another supervisor, so I'm your girl for the summer."

She had a crisp, breezy demeanor that was somehow still warm, and it put me at ease. It made me feel like I had known her for much longer than five minutes.

Sonia clapped her hands together and smiled at me.

"First things first, let's get you settled into your new desk. I've been keeping it warm for you."

She hopped off the desk and onto her slingbacks, and I couldn't help but laugh a little. I tentatively set my purse down on the desk, angling the scuffed side away from Sonia.

"The space is yours to use as you see fit, but I don't expect you'll be getting a lot of use out of it."

"Oh?" I asked, confused.

Sonia wound a finger through one of her impossibly tight ringlet curls. They framed her face in a thick bob, dark chestnut shot through with a honey highlight that set off her golden skin.

"You'll probably be on your feet most of the time, running memos back and forth, running errands, taking dictation, making coffee, that sort of thing. The classic New York intern experience. Mr. Thorpe keeps us all busy here, and the new hires are no exception."

There was that name again. Like most people with a working television, I heard it before. I heard it more than I wanted to living with two straight women and one bisexual man who liked to complain he was single and that none of them had a shot with a guy like Thorpe. Luke Thorpe was the darling of the tech world, a wunderkind who had launched SkyBlue out of his college dorm room on a shoestring budget and somehow propelled it to a market value in the billions. Supposedly Thorpe himself was worth a billion, shocking for anyone, but particularly someone who was only thirty-two. I had heard the swooning spiel before from my roommate Joannah. I just never thought I would be this close to the subject of her fantasies.

"I've heard he's pretty demanding," I ventured carefully. Demanding didn't even begin to cover what the press had to say about him. They said he was a single-minded machine who pushed his employees to the point of exhaustion in the pursuit of excellence. No one had brought action against him for negligence, and SkyBlue employees were lavished with absurd pay and benefits, but people knew that anyone who worked in the gleaming glass building had to be performing optimally at all times to meet Thorpe's standards. Peter, Joanna's boyfriend, ribbed me about it that morning while we were brushing our teeth in the cramped single bathroom the four of us shared, insisting that I was going to drop from exhaustion on the subway ride home after my first day. But I could see concern underneath his bravado, and it made me concerned too.

Sonia smiled. A little, tightly I thought.

"We have a pretty uptight company culture sometimes, it's true, but we know how to let off steam as well. I'll make sure you get invited to one of the after-work happy hours. It's when we get together and have vodka lemonades and unwind from the workweek."

"That sounds nice. I guess I should be on my best behavior at all times then, huh?"

It was an attempt at a joke, one that I hoped didn't sound spoiled or lazy, but Sonia seemed to sense my real question.

"This isn't a Devil Wears Prada situation, Emily, and Thorpe's no Meryl Streep. You'll work your ass off here, I won't lie about that, but you'll be treated like an adult and your off hours will be respected. If anyone gives you any trouble, you send them to me. Don't worry about Thorpe. I know how to handle him.

"Will I be working with him at all?" I couldn't decide if I was excited by the prospect or terrified. Sonia waved my question away with a laugh.

"Almost certainly not. The only one who can get an audience with the guy, much less get through to him, is Olivia. You'll meet her. She's his secretary, but so much more than that, she keeps us all sane, I think. No, interns pretty much never interact with the CEO directly.

"Ah," I said, trying not to sound disappointed. While I wasn't excited by the idea of throwing myself at Thorpe's feet and begging for his approval, I knew a recommendation letter penned by him would mean a lot more than one written by well-meaning Sonia. She didn't need to know that right then, however. I didn't think it looked good to admit that you had only taken a job for the resume experience on your first day.

"I'll leave you to get settled in," Sonia said, standing and breezing past me. I caught the scent of her resinous, heady perfume, thick with plums and iris and other notes too elevated for my Bath & Body Works nose to pick up. "I'll be back around in twenty to give you a tour of the office. Congrats again, Emily. We're happy to have you."

I smiled as she drifted away, and only then realized I had my fingernails pressed into the palms of my hands, so they hard were leaving half-moon imprints. When had I ever been this nervous? It was going to take all the nerves I had left to get through the day. But I would get through it. And the next day and the next day, if I wanted to bring home my share of the rent and keep any hope of Paris alive. I had to.

PREQUEL

*H*ave you read the FREE Prequel to "Beauty and the BOSS" yet? If not, you can download this at below link

Click HERE to Download the FREE Prequel

Chapter Three

LUKE

I took a deep sip from my cappuccino, rifling through the folders Olivia laid out neatly on my desk that morning. It was all information relating to a new partnership SkyBlue was forging with a sizeable domestic car company, one that could make our technology more accessible to the average consumer without sacrificing quality. It was the kind of collaborative sponsorship deal I had dreamed of since I was twenty, doodling fast cars in the margins of my chemistry notebook. I had been angling for it hard in the past year, doing everything I could to beat out our Swedish competitor. Getting the contract had been like securing a sought-after heiress in marriage, and I should be feeling happier about it now. But at the moment, all I could think of was the flurry of press conferences I would be expected to attend and the headache of paperwork that would be following me for months. And, of course, the pointed expectation from our manufacturing partner that the inclusion of top-of-the-line

SkyBlue tech in their luxury sedans would boost profit margins to an ungodly number. I had made big promises in pursuing this deal, and now I had to keep them.

The first time my phone rang, I ignored it, opting instead to glance back at the prototype specs of the sedan that would be shown at a high-end automotive event next week. The second time, I snapped it up to my face and sighed,

"I'm working, Sarah."

"Surprise, surprise," my sister said. "Although I guess I can't nag you about it too much since it is a weekday. Do you have a minute?"

"Not really."

"Just a minute, Luke, I promise. Ryan is here too! He wants to say hello to his uncle. Ryan, can you say hello to Uncle Luke?"

Ryan trumpeted out his greeting from somewhere in the room behind her, singsonging over my name with a child's unashamed exuberance. A smile tugged at the corners of my mouth before I smothered it. Sarah knew how to get to me. And she wouldn't be calling at this hour unless she wanted something.

"What is it?" I asked, trying to sound genuinely interested and not testy.

"Actually, dad's here! He'd like to talk to you for a second."

"Sarah," I began warningly, but before I could protest, I had been passed from my sister to my father. I very rarely took calls from him even when I was free. I wouldn't put it past the sly old dog to ask my sister to dial on his behalf. He didn't respect the healthy boundaries I set between us very well. It wasn't that I hated him, or that we were constantly at odds. We just had very different perspectives, and I had never managed to regain the respect I lost for him when he had turned to drinking in those first few years after my mother's death. College was a relief; it gave me time to establish myself as my own man, and he took the time to pull himself together.

"Luke," My father began in his gravelly voice. "How are things?"

"Just fine dad. What's going on?"

"Well, we were just sitting around here talking about how long it's been since we were all together."

I bristled. "Who's 'all?'"

"Just the family. Sarah and Ryan and Eric."

Anger came up in my throat, metallic tasting, and I couldn't help the sneer that twisted my mouth.

"Sarah didn't mention Venom was there."

"*Luke,*" My father chided, so harshly it came out almost as a bark. It sounded like his face was well on its way to deep red with fury, a shade I often saw when I was around him. The man had a shorter fuse than a grenade, and we always seemed to rub each other the wrong way.

"Sorry, I meant Vernon. A slip of the tongue."

"I've about had it up to here with your bad attitude. You never call anymore, never come out to eat with us, and then you act like this as soon as I get you on the phone?"

I sighed deeply, dredging up an apology, or at least an attempt at one, from deep within me. But before I could get a word in edgewise, my father continued with his barrage.

"What about forgiveness, Luke? It's been damn near five years. Everyone else is over it, we've all moved on, as a family. Are you a part of this family, or aren't you?"

I could hear a low, worried murmur in the background. It sounded like Sarah exchanging words with Eric. Anger bubbled up inside me all over again at the thought of them whispering about me. Eric always had some inane opinion that Sarah would softly try to dissuade him from. I don't know why he even both-ered pretending to like me in the first place since it was obvious there was no love lost between us now.

"Of course I'm part of the family," I said smoothly. "I was just with Sarah and everyone a few days ago."

"I heard about that," my father said, settling somewhat. I could almost hear his blood pressure going down, slowly but surely. "Sarah said it was good to get you out of that office."

"It wasn't terrible, I'll admit. It was nice to spend time with Ryan and the family."

"See? You've just gotta put yourself out there more."

"Maybe."

"Listen, we'd like you to come out to dinner with us."

"When?"

"Tonight!"

"Tonight? Dad, I'm working tonight."

"You're always working nights."

"Yes, well, that's what needs to be done. And I went out just the other night, I've seen Sarah and Ryan and even Eric, alright? You know our time together is valuable to me, but I've got a company to run here. We've got this sponsorship deal and this huge launch in a few months and I can't—"

"I'm so tired of hearing about this launch! There are always going to be launches, Luke. But we're your family, and we might not always be here! Ryan won't be seven forever."

"Don't bring Ryan into this," I said, my voice dropping to a low, steely pitch. If my father was trying to arouse my ire and land himself in my black books, he was well on his way. "Don't use him as leverage, alright? I'll think about it. But don't get your hopes up."

"Luke—" My father began. I hung up before he could do

anything else to infuriate me. There was a light knock at my door.

"What?" I snapped, then immediately regretted it. It was my secretary, Oliva, one of the best things that ever happened to my company or me. In addition to being an essential component of my work life, she was also a dear friend and was one of the few people I would take the time to get an after-work cocktail with from time to time. Granted, we usually ended up talking about work, but she could often make me laugh in the process, and I appreciated that.

"Who pissed in your coffee?" She asked dryly. She was wearing a crimson dress that set off her tawny skin and her jet black hair hung in loose in waves.

"My father," I said, kneading my brow.

"Oh! How is Marty?"

"Still a bastard."

"Got it. Well." She shifted the notebooks she was carrying on her hip, then crossed over to the desk and set them down in front of me. Then she flipped through a few pages on a clipboard. "Ready for the week's rundown?"

"It's Monday, isn't it?"

"I'll take that as a yes."

Olivia launched into the week's events in her crisp, professional tones. I had them all marked down already, in online calendars and memos and email reminders, but I liked to hear her lay it all out for me at the start of the week. It was one of my little secrets to success that Forbes columnists were always hounding me to share. Arianna Huffington had her bubble baths. I had my weekly check-ins.

"As you can tell, it's going to be a doozy of a week," Olivia finished. "But I've spaced everything with as much breathing room as I could find to give you, which is to say: not much."

"What about the press?"

"What about them?"

"They'll want statements, photo-ops, that kind of thing."

Olivia pursed her bright red lips at me, pulling her brows together in confusion.

"Luke, you're completely booked. Slammed, even. There's no way..."

"Call a press conference for Thursday. Just a small one, I'm sure we can find the time."

"And the prototype presentations on Thursday?"

"I'll go to those too. Come to think of it; I want an advance showing before we get all the investors in here. Just to make sure everything is ready to go. Maybe Tuesday? Hell, I'll do it today if the manufacturers are ready."

Olivia sighed heavily. She didn't argue with me about pacing myself or delegating to others; she knew me too well for that. Instead, she asked, "When will you sleep?"

I threw back the rest of my cappuccino, already flipping through the mountains of material Oliva had brought in for my perusal and approval.

"Sleep is overrated."

Chapter Four
EMILY

*A*fter a week of working six hours days at SkyBlue that somehow felt more like twelve, I still felt like I was drowning in new information, but I was getting a better hold on processing it. The job description hadn't been lying when it said "other duties as needs arise." I nearly ran holes in my shoes scurrying up and down the hallways of SkyBlue, dropping off folders, answering phones, picking up steaming trays of coffee, and hurriedly scribbling notes in meetings. Even though my shorter day as an intern left me with plenty of time in the evening to socialize with my roommates, I got into the habit of making an early dinner and unwinding with an hour of Netflix in my room before falling asleep. Morning and the long train ride into Midtown came all too soon every day, but I stuck at it, and slowly but surely, I started to get a handle on things. I began to intuit the rhythm of an average work day and match names to faces.

In particular, Sonia and Olivia were becoming something like friends to me, and they would often smile at me and open up their tight conversation to welcome me in as a third while we brewed coffee in the tiny staff kitchen. This was the perfect time, of course, to swap gossip, and I found myself more up to date on company tabloid rumors than most other interns.

Luke Thorpe was, of course, an evergreen topic. Olivia used her frequent coffee refill trips to complain about how meticulous he was, and how he was working himself into the ground. They seemed to be on a first name basis, and she certainly bad-mouthed him more than most assistants did their bosses, but it seemed to come from a place of love. To me, it seemed almost sisterly, the bristling irritation mixed with genuine care. Sonia was always happy to listen, and usually had an opinion or two to interject about Luke's jam-packed schedule or his appearance in the glossy pages of magazines. I had never met Luke, so I hadn't formed an opinion of him yet. I wondered if I ever would.

"It's not that he's doing poorly," Olivia said one day, stirring a generous helping of sweet creamer into her coffee. "Hell, he's doing better than most people I know. The man gets up at five, exercises five days a week, and outpaces everyone at work. But there's more to life than business achievements. I'm just worried about his work-life balance."

Sonia snorted into her cup of decaf.

"That man doesn't know the meaning of work-life balance."

"Is he always like that?" I asked. Generally, at our little lunch hour rendezvous, I just smiled and listened, but I had started feeling bold enough to ask a few questions. "Or is it just because of the launch?"

Olivia rolled her eyes.

"If it weren't the product launch, it would be something else. He's always got an excuse for working late. I don't think he'd know what to do with any time off in that big empty condo of his. The man hasn't taken a vacation in five years. Five!"

Sonia whistled lowly, then said with a smirk,

"Well, whatever he's doing, overworking seems to agree with him. I swear every time I see him, he gets hotter. Did you see the suit he was wearing today, that matte black number? Made me swoon. He looks like a bad-tempered James Bond."

"Oh, keep it to yourself, Sonia."

"What, am I supposed to pretend to be blind? Listen, if Luke Thorpe were willing to look up from his work and pay attention to a woman for five seconds, I would be making a fool of myself trying to get his attention. Don't tell me you haven't noticed. You're always alone in that office with him."

"I've known Luke since we were eighteen; he brought me into the company in its infancy. We trust each other. We're friends."

"So, you have noticed."

Olivia sighed heavily, but it looked like she was trying to cover up a girlish smile when she brought her coffee cup to her lips.

"Alright, I've noticed. There's nothing saying I can't admire fine craftsmanship if I see it. But I don't want Luke. Not the way you're thinking."

"Well I'm not afraid to say I do," Sonia said breezily. "Do you think he likes brunettes?"

I must have made a little scoffing sound into my mug of tea because Sonia's eyes flickered over to me.

"Full of opinions today?" She asked breezily. As far as I could tell she wasn't really angry, maybe just a little riled, but still friendly, which was a good thing considering she was my immediate supervisor. But she hadn't exactly been conducting herself in a particularly professional way during this conversation, so I didn't feel bad about my attitude.

"It's just that every woman in the office seems to love him."

"He's handsome, he's rich, he's single, and he loves kids," Olivia said with a shrug. "Objectively, he's a catch."

"And he's got those scold-me-Daddy-I've-been-bad eyes," Sonia said wistfully, half lost in her own fantasy. Olivia swatted her, shooting me a scandalized look.

"You're on the job, Sonia."

"Hey, at least I'm honest. Am I wrong?"

"That's not up for discussion. Let's talk about something else. Luke would have a fit if he heard this."

"That sounds good to me," I put in, feeling a little relieved. While I liked to gossip, I was still getting used to Sonia's forthrightness. I got the sense that she was a hard nut to crack, but if she decided she liked you and invited you into her social circle, she was no-holds-barred about speaking her mind.

"Fine, fine," Sonia said. Then she nodded to the glossy leather handbag Olivia had brought with her into the kitchen, the one patterned with black and brown checks. "Let's talk about that new Louis bag. Is it the Neverfull?"

Olivia's face lit up in pure girlish joy, and she took up the bag and held it to her chest. "Yes! An early birthday present to myself. I have the larger one, but I thought the medium size would be perfect for everyday use and look! I got the Rose Ballerine interior. Isn't it such a pretty color?"

Sonia nodded her approval. I had been struggling to memorize the little logos that gave away the designer goods so many of the women wore to work and gushed over with each other like hunting trophies. But the Chanel and Gucci symbols were still too similar for me to tell apart, and so were Louis Vuitton and

Yves Saint Laurent. Even worse, I was sure that if I tried to pronounce any of their names, I would butcher them. Better to keep quiet then, and not admit that I hadn't been raised in a household where anyone would ever consider spending three thousand dollars on a bag, even if we had it.

Part of me still felt that investing so much money in an accessory was ridiculous, but another part of me knew that I should probably put more effort into my presentation. There had to be a happy medium somewhere between my patchy drugstore eyeshadow and flimsy Rue21 tops and Sonia's vintage designer boots, or Olivia's rotating wardrobe of Calvin Klein dresses. I just wasn't sure how to find my way there. My mother hadn't been concerned with her outward appearance, favoring functionality over fashion. She wore a plain suit to work most days. I taught myself to shop by the lowest price point, not by quality. Self-consciously, I glanced down at the tight knit dress I was wearing. The hem was work appropriate, but the material was paper thin jersey that probably was better suited to pajamas, and my blazer, boxy, and one size too large was rescued from my mother's closet.

Olivia must have caught me looking at myself because she stopped gloating about her bag and set it on the counter again, looking a little pink in the cheeks.

"Of course I never would have bought something like this when I was first starting at this job," she said, probably more for my benefit than for Sonia's.

"Oh yeah, of course," Sonia said, catching her drift and following her gaze over to me. "Hey, Emily, your shoes are really pretty!"

"Thanks," I mumbled. I was terrible at taking compliments even when it didn't feel like they were being given as a consolation prize. These dark cherry lacquered slingbacks had been a high school graduation gift from my grandmother. Somehow, the compliment stung more, knowing that I hadn't picked these shoes, much less bought them, myself.

"Learning how to dress for a new job is always hard," Olivia said soothingly. "Every office is different, and it isn't always clear from the interview what you need."

"Yeah, I don't think at first I..." I gulped tea to soothe my nerves. "Really realized how formally people dress around here."

"It's not your fault; It's Luke's. Tech startups are notoriously casual, so it's okay if that's more what you were expecting. Luke is just... he likes things done to the nines. And he sets a sort of example for us all to follow."

"I'm learning that. I'm just not that into clothes, you know?"

This wasn't strictly true. I saw dresses in shop windows that took my breath away every day and was just as enchanted by beautiful color, a swirl of interesting fabric, or a sharp cut of tailoring as the next person. I just never let myself try them on once I saw the price tag, and I convinced myself that Goodwill and the clearance rack at Target were good enough for a college sophomore with an absurd amount of student debt.

"There are some great thrift shops in this part of the city where you can get really nice pieces at a discount. You'd be surprised at how far a couple of basics can get you! You can never go wrong with neutrals, either; they never clash."

I smiled weakly at the fashion advice. It was good advice and given kindly, but I hadn't asked for it, and it felt uncomfortably close to my supervisor telling me to put in a little more effort.

"I'll check it out, thanks."

Sonia looked at me sympathetically and opened her mouth to say something, but then the door to Luke's office flew open.

From our vantage point in the tiny kitchen, we could see across a row of cubicles to Luke's corner office, and he could see in here as well if he thought to glance over.

"Shit," Sonia swore and dropped into a crouch. Olivia followed a heartbeat later and tugged me down after her. I wasn't expecting any of this and ended up collapsed into a heap on the floor.

"What's going on?" I asked in a hissed whisper. The back of my calves burned from squatting down in high heels.

"Just avoiding the wrath of Thorpe," Sonia said. "He doesn't like it when we burn company time gossiping, but I would argue they should include it in the mental health section of our benefits package."

Olivia pushed herself up just a bit, casting a glance around the room before ducking back down again.

"Doesn't look like he's out hunting for either of us. He just went into the CFO's office."

"Poor Carl. Do you want to write his obituary, or should I?"

Sonia and Olivia both devolved into giggles and snickers, and I wondered, not for the first time, how in the world I had gotten myself into this.

Chapter Five

LUKE

I didn't bother with pleasantries or greetings when I let myself into Carl's office.

"Tell me you have good news for me," I said, tossing a folder down on his desk. "Do not tell me you made me get up from what I was doing and come all the way over here for bad news."

Carl looked up from his computer, a little startled. Like Oliva, Carl had been with SkyBlue since the earliest days of the company, and I appointed him my CFO when we were still just two kids sleeping in a dorm room and trying to scrape together enough money for ramen noodles. He always believed in my work and was loyal to a fault, but he moved a little too slowly for me. From idea to idea, from place to place, from our shared bathroom in the morning when I needed to shave and get to work. He was annoyingly fond of face-to-face interactions over more efficient emails or texts and always asked me over to "pick my brain" or "run things by me" in person.

"Hi to you too. I feel like I haven't seen you all week. You alright? And what are you talking about? All the way over here? You work three doors down."

"Close enough. You've got five minutes. What's up?"

Carl leaned back in his chair and took his reading glasses off, agonizingly slowly. He was only two years older than me, and he was getting prematurely farsighted from staring at tiny data points all day. Otherwise, he still looked the way he did when we were in college: square New England accent, tousled reddish-brown curls, and a smattering of freckles that somehow didn't make him look childish. His brown eyes were far too kind for his own good. Between the two of us, people usually preferred talking to Carl and generally introduced themselves to him first. Something about my demeanor being "cold" and "off-putting." But they also tried to wheedle him with sob stories or press him for a bigger cut of the budget, and worst of all, he often heard them out. I had never been able to teach him how to cut people off before they could ask for something.

"Listen, I've been thinking about this new partnership, and how it might affect our five-year plan as a company."

"Sounds like this conversation could have been an email."

"Just one minute, hear me out." Carl steepled his fingers and fixed me with a weighted look. "I've been thinking about a subscription service."

"A what?"

"A subscription service. Everyone's got them now, and they're doing gangbusters."

"Carl, we're a car company, not a box of useless shit that gets delivered to your door every month."

"No, no, that's not the kind of thing I'm talking about!" He waved my words away like they were smoke and leaned forward across his desk. I could tell from the gleam in his eye that he might be on to something, the lightning insight that came to him after he mulled things over for a month or two. So I let him go on. "What's the biggest problem in the tech industry right now?"

"God, do you want a list?"

"I mean from the consumer perspective. Your average Joe on the street with a smartphone. Come on; take a guess."

I thought it over for a minute.

"Planned obsolescence?"

Carl slapped his desk in triumph.

"Exactly! You buy a phone, and it lasts two years before it starts fritzing out on you; you buy a car, and it lasts five years, maybe, if you're lucky. The higher tech something is, the shorter its lifespan because software systems go out of date, replacement parts are pricey, and people stop being trained to service whatever has gone out of style. Makes tech manufacturers a ton of money. Everybody knows we do it; nobody knows a way around it."

I wasn't entirely following at this point. I crossed my arms and furrowed my brows.

"The way around it is to downgrade your purchases, buy a new phone, or trade in your car. We make a lot of money on those trade-ins as you said, and at any rate, tech advances too fast for anything to stay relevant for long. iPods were revolutionary a decade ago; now look at them."

"Exactly. So what if there was a way to keep people from downgrading to cheaper cars and ensuring that they signed on to the newest SkyBlue release while saving them money in the long run?"

"You know I hate rhetorical questions; tell me or don't."

"I'm thinking about introducing an exclusive package deal

that customers can opt into when they purchase a vehicle equipped with SkyBlue technology. This subscription service would give them advance access to the newest SkyBlue models at a discounted price, and, most importantly, give them yearly tech upgrades in their current vehicle at no additional cost. No more losing your GPS because it's not compatible with new operating systems or swapping your car because suddenly the automated driving functions are outdated."

"Doesn't that seem a little generous to you? I feel like we would lose money. What would our margins be on a model like that?"

"Very cushy. People are paying for security and convenience. It doesn't cost us anywhere near the subscription fee to upgrade the vehicles. And more than that, it creates brand loyalty. It shows we're committed to keeping our customers up to date with the best. You've seen the satisfaction numbers same as me. People are afraid of signing on to such new technology, and they're afraid it will get outdated just as soon as they've become comfortable with it. We can't rely on sales to early adopters forever. Eventually, we need to attract soccer moms and suburban commuters and parents looking to get a safe car for their college freshman."

I ran my hand over my well-trimmed stubble, thinking intently. I was aware I was probably scowling, which was one of my most common expressions, but Carl wasn't deterred. I had never been able to intimidate him, which was one of the reasons he remained so valuable to me. Carl was the real deal, even if he annoyed me like no one else.

"You've got reservations," he noted.

"A few," I admitted.

"Let's hear them."

"I would have to see specs. And numbers. I want to know the exact cost of rolling out a service like this, and the cost if it fails."

"Oh, I know. I'm already having the boys in R&D draft something up to send to you. What else?"

"Carl, this is a luxury company. By nature and design. We offer the best of the best to people, and I'm not sure how something as mass-market as a subscription service would affect our company image."

Carl sighed heavily.

"All you ever did in college was talk about how you wanted SkyBlue automation to be available in every car in the country and accessible to any buyer with money to spend."

"I still do," I said defensively. "I think self-driving cars are the future. They're safe and practical and—"

"I've heard the spiel, and I get it. You know I believe in it too. So why are you so afraid of losing that luxury status? We won't, Luke, the products speak for itself. And to be quite honest, we still price out most buyers. Reaching down into the middle class a bit will not hurt us. If you really believe in accessibility, you have to be willing to make things accessible. End of story. And to be quite frank with you, our sales are plateauing. We're on track to start losing money in three years if nothing changes. I think this is a great way forward."

I straightened my cuffs, brows still furrowed in deep thought. I remembered being ten and being bullied by the bigger boys in my neighborhood because my shoes came from Walmart and had filthy frayed laces that desperately needed to be replaced. And being fifteen, ogling my neighbor's refinished muscle car when I knew I didn't have enough money for a bus pass. I worked so hard to not only become rich but appear rich, learning how to dress and speak, sip wine, and listen to conversations about the stock market. Everyone already knew I was new money, and the tiniest slip could expose me as nothing more than a ratty, poor kid from the Queens with a bloated bank account. But that was my damage, my issue. I couldn't project that onto my company, especially not when it went against the ethos that underpinned my mission here.

"I'm not saying yes. But I'll think about it."

"Good," Carl said, sighing out the word with relief. "I've got plenty for you to go over, but I know you've got a full week. Thursday work alright for you?"

"Send it over whenever you like, I don't care."

Carl arched an eyebrow.

"You sound more irritable than usual. Is everything alright? Olivia said you haven't been sleeping."

I gave him a withering glance and reminded myself to let Olivia know exactly what I thought of her discussing my personal life outside the office later.

"Olivia needs to keep her opinions to herself. I'm fine, Carl."

"Talked to your brother-in-law lately?"

"I don't know, have you talked to your ex-wife? Or are the two of you still just estranged? I'm assuming they'll award her custody of Lisa."

The words came out acidic, more biting than I meant to be with an old friend, and I knew Carl had been right about the stress getting to me. A shadow passed over his face, and he put his reading glasses back on, turning from me slightly to look back at his screen.

"You're an asshole," he muttered, half-hearted because he had told me so many times.

"I know," I said. What else was there to say?

Carl didn't glance at me when he spoke again.

"As I said, I'll have something sent over. Sorry for taking up so much of your time."

I wanted to do something, to rewind the last five minutes and steer the conversation towards more productive waters, but instead, I stormed out of his office and into my own without another word.

I spent the rest of the day in a rotten mood, irritated with every new email that popped into my inbox and snapping at Olivia about her mouth when she came in at two pm with my afternoon espresso. She icily told me that my two thirty appointment was waiting and that she would not be waiting for me after work for our planned happy hour with Carl. This did not improve my mood.

I wanted not to care. I wanted to turn on that machine personality that everyone in the press insisted I had and plow through Carl's feelings, and Olivia's. They had irritated me, after all, and should know better than to interfere with the tight ship I liked to run. But there was a tiny voice in my head reminding me that these were my friends, two of the oldest and most loyal ones I had, after the boys from the neighborhood where I grew up. No one understood SkyBlue like them, or my vision for the company, or my eccentricities as a CEO. There was being an asshole as expected, and there was isolating the people closest to me when I needed them most. I felt that I had, potentially, blurred those lines a little too much that day.

I stopped by Carl's office after I clocked out for the day. He was still at work, crunching numbers while the sun set behind him. I knocked twice and didn't bother waiting for a response before poking my head in.

"Hi," I said, a little quieter than usual.

Carl glanced up, then saw who it was and looked back down at his work, the corners of his mouth tightening.

"Need something, Luke?"

"Are you coming out? It's six thirty."

"I don't think so. I've got a lot on my plate tonight."

"We all do. Come on; we only do this once a month. Let me make it up to you with a drink."

This got his attention, no matter how much he wanted to look calm and unaffected.

"Make it up to me? Is the impassive Luke Thorpe actually apologizing for something?"

"Of course not. I'm offering to buy you a drink. That's all. Take it or leave it."

Carl sighed heavily, but a small smile appeared on his face. At the end of the day, we were the closest thing to brothers each other had.

"Alright. I'll take you up on that."

"Olivia isn't coming."

"Oh, I know. Get her a Frappuccino tomorrow, and she'll forgive you."

"We'll see," I said, then jangled my car keys at Carl. "You've got five minutes to wrap things up, or I'm leaving you behind."

I ducked out before I could get pulled into a conversation with more emotional substance, leaving him to decide whether he would take me up on my offer. I like to think that by now, we understood each other's idiosyncrasies and spoke the same nonverbal language. It was that sort of sync that made us a good team, especially in an industry where CEOs and CFOs often butted heads or even vied for each other's authority.

By six thirty the building had emptied out, and the only employees left at their desks were those with catch-up to play or overtime to log. Some of them glanced my way and then quickly dropped their eyes back to their keyboards. I tended to have that effect on people. Olivia was long gone, her screen dark, the pile of post-it notes she kept her day's running to-do list on neatly discarded. She sometimes poked her head in near the end of her workday to ask if I wanted her to get the ball rolling on anything before she headed out, but not today.

Maybe Carl's idea about a Frappuccino hadn't been a bad idea after all.

I made a beeline for the elevator, weaving through cubicles on the most expedient route. A woman with long red hair pulled into a braid had just stepped inside, and I caught the door with my hand moments before it closed. As the elevator door dinged and slid open, her eyes widened in surprise.

The woman in the elevator was a head shorter than me but had an impressive figure, with a lean frame and delicate collar bones exposed by the boat neckline on her shirt. Her eyes were an arresting blue, her red mouth set in a hard, worried line. She was stunning in a short hemline, and a flush bloomed across her cheeks. She was also the girl who got carjacked on the side of the road a few months ago. The one who haunted my mind every free moment I had. The one I thought I would never see again.

I got into the elevator and pressed the lobby button. That gave us thirteen floors together, maybe two minutes of a second chance for me to make the right first impression.

I wanted to introduce myself, to remind her of that night, but just as I turned to speak to her, she lost her grip on the stacks of papers she was holding and ducked down to retrieve the runaways, her face flaring red. She was nervous, way more than she should be in the elevator with another working professional. I stooped down beside her to help her gather up her papers, but she flinched back when I reached towards her hand. Just a bit, but I saw it, and I saw the tightening of her shoulders. Was she afraid? It certainly seemed like she was holding back fear, working hard to keep herself composed as much as she could. What was the problem?

The answer hit me in the face. The carjacking, you idiot. She was carjacked by two men who cornered her at gunpoint. She probably wouldn't be very excited about someone she thought was a stranger moving into her personal space in a cramped, isolated elevator.

In the end, I opted not to bring up that night, which must have been so terrible for her, and I didn't touch her. But I did hand back one of the packets of paper that slid over to my side of the elevator, which, to my surprise, turned out to be the SkyBlue employee handbook.

"Thank you," she said quietly, not meeting my eyes. Her face was half-hidden in a curtain of fiery hair.

Had she been working here the entire time? No, I would have noticed her by now, the company was still small enough that I was introduced to all of our full-time employees at least once. As I had intuited the night we met, she was quite young, probably not out of college yet, and was most likely one of our summer interns.

Sonia would know, but we didn't often communicate directly. Interns weren't my business after I looked over the applications and interviewer's notes to give my final approval. Most other CEOs would see this as a gross misuse of my time, but I like to know the kind of people we welcomed into our doors, and I liked to make sure that they seemed like the type who could meet SkyBlue's rigorous standards. If an intern had a nervous breakdown two months into their stint and required us to hire and re-train an entirely new person, it would cost the company time and money, which I wouldn't stand for.

I wracked my brain to remember the mountain of applications I had flipped through a few months ago, and the names on them. Emily was a name I remembered, but I couldn't recall if she had been one of the applicants I approved. She must have been, though, because here she was. Right under my roof all along.

I wondered if she was so nervous because she recognized me as her rescuer and was putting the pieces together that I was also her boss. But then I remembered that I had never taken off my helmet. She would have to have an excellent memory to pull that whole picture together, and the entire night was probably a blur to her. As much as I wanted to confess, I decided not to spring that on her just yet. If she worked in my building, I would have plenty of time to interact with her in my future, especially if I made it my business to.

"First day?" I asked lightly.

Those pale blue eyes darted up at me, almost in shock. Did she recognize my voice? That would do the heavy lifting of my letting her in on what I knew for me. But then she glanced away, looking a little confused, and I knew my voice hadn't landed for her. Not entirely.

"Oh, no, but I'm new. I've only been here a few weeks."

She smiled nervously, and I smiled back down at her, as warmly and indulgently as I could. She opened her mouth to say something else, the color rising deliciously in her cheeks, but then the elevator dinged, as though it were a chaperone at a school dance.

"Nice to meet you," she mumbled, and then zipped out of the elevator before we could exchange another word. I watched her dart through the throng of people in the lobby before disappearing out the glass doors and jogging across the street to the subway station. She wasn't exactly running away, but she certainly wasn't wasting any time either.

I stepped out of the elevator in a bit of a daze, running a hand over the back of my neck. The odds of ever seeing Emily again, much less having her show up as an intern at my company, were lottery-winning. More than that. If I didn't know better, I would think I was being set up by one of those hidden camera shows. But she had been in that elevator with me, real and radiating warmth and that sugary mall perfume that intoxicated me the night we first met. She had been slipping in and out of my daydreams and my nighttime fantasies for months, the perfect picture of what I desired, and it had gotten to the point where I wondered if I had made the whole night with the carjacking up. But here she was within reach.

My phone buzzed, and I glanced down at the text from Carl. He wanted to know what time we were meeting at the bar, and if I felt like eating dinner or not. I couldn't bring myself to care to answer, not immediately anyway. Instead, I went out to my car, moving at a brisk clip, and sat there in silence in the parking garage for a long minute.

"Emily," I muttered to myself, amazed at her very existence. There had to be something to this. If I felt this strongly about someone I hardly knew, we had to have some spark of intense connection. And I was fully set on using my laser-focused determination to act on that spark when the moment was right.

Chapter Six
EMILY

I couldn't believe how fast I rushed out of that elevator without even looking him in the eye. I kept replaying the moment over and over again as I languished on my tiny twin bed. Just as I had the entire subway ride home from work, it was like my brain had just evaporated as soon as those elevator doors closed behind us. I couldn't tell if the panic was from being in an enclosed space with a man for the first time since being dragged from my car by a gunman, or because the man was Luke Thorpe. Because Luke was, up close, even more mind-meltingly handsome than he was from fifteen feet away. Maybe it was both.

And more than that, there was something about him that got under my skin, something that I couldn't shake. It wasn't just that he was handsome, tall and sharp-jawed and certainly well built underneath that suit. He towered over my 5'4 frame, and I expected he was at least 5'10 if not a full six feet. No wonder everyone in the office seemed drawn to him. But there was something more to him, something that reminded me of someone I couldn't quite place. I was sure we hadn't met before; I would remember an encounter with my boss. But still, he seemed strangely familiar, and my body responded to him as though we knew each other more intimately. His touch had burned against my skin when he reached out to help me gather the papers I had spilled in a fit of nerves, and it had felt like an almost sexual transgression of personal space, one I wasn't ready for. But that didn't mean I hadn't enjoyed it if I was completely honest with myself.

Still, the way he sized me up implied that I had no idea what I was doing. It was insulting, infuriatingly so. He asked me if it was my first day. Why did he think it was okay to say that to someone who just spilled papers and notes everywhere? Was this the man I was supposed to win over and convince to write me a glowing recommendation to the summer program in Paris?

"Asshole," I muttered to myself, but even I knew that was half-hearted. I kicked up the plastic fan whirring at the end of my bed another notch. Summer in the city was brutal. I couldn't afford an apartment with AC, and I was suddenly feeling hot in my face and neck.

My phone rang, and I leaned off the side of my bed to pull it out of my purse, which lay discarded where I dropped it as soon as I arrived home. It was my mother again. She had been calling more frequently over the past few weeks. Maybe trying to reconnect with her daughter living away from home for the first time, or perhaps because she was still worried about me after the carjacking. I considered answering, then rejected her call. I was still feeling mixed-up and jittery from the elevator ride and didn't feel like talking.

The air from the fan stirred the hair around my face as I sat ruminating furiously about the elevator incident while gnawing on my thumbnail. He had looked at me in such an intense way, like he wanted to know me better, or like he already knew me. But that was impossible, wasn't it? I was just an intern. We had never been introduced, and I never so much as made eye contact with Luke Thorpe until today. The more I tried to put him out of my mind, the more preoccupied I became with him, until I found myself, to my great embarrassment, scrolling through press photos of him on my phone twenty minutes later. I should just put him out of my mind and go on with my business. But there was no forgetting his powerful presence next to me in that elevator, or the way his watery, woodsy cologne had smelled like money and the beach and the leather interior of an expensive car.

Maybe it was this indulgent spree of Googling and dreaming that led me to be so bold the next morning and do something I would never have otherwise dreamed of.

It started because Olivia was having a stressful day. Well, more stressful than usual it seemed, from the way she stabbed at the keyboard on her computer, snapped at people on the phone, and kneaded her brows with a sigh every few minutes. Everyone was working overtime to prepare for the new product launch, and we were all feeling the push, but I suppose Olivia got the worst of it as the CEO's personal assistant. When I walked over to her desk to deliver some photocopies from another department, she hardly glanced up at me, and her smile, usually so sunny and encouraging, was thin. She looked like she hadn't slept in days, and there were crumpled breakfast sandwich wrappers and a half-empty Venti Frappuccino on her desk. This wouldn't be too strange for anyone else, but I had seen Olivia taking perfectly portioned, healthy home-cooked lunches out of the staff kitchen fridge more than once. The launch had taken over her life.

"Thank you," she said and struggled to find a place for the papers on her overcrowded desk. She shoved a few things aside, then went looking for something else of importance while I stood awkwardly with my fingers laced. "Just one second, I have... Let me give you this while you're here. Ugh, where did they go?"

I said nothing while she swore to herself and flipped through papers and folders. Eventually, she found a sales sheet with a crumpled edge that she thrust into my hands.

"This goes to Carl, please, and thank you. He might have errands for you as well, so just check while you're in — oh fuck." She had just glanced over at her desk clock and noticed, with a pale expression, the time. "It's almost two. Shit, I forgot Luke's espresso. I'm so busy, and it just fell right through the cracks..."

She pushed herself up from her desk, talking to herself more than me, and an impulsive idea welled up inside me.

"I can take Mr. Thorpe his coffee."

She blinked at me as though I wasn't speaking English.

"What?"

"It looks like you've got a lot on your plate right now. Delivering coffee is an intern thing, right? I'm happy to run out for you and—"

She sagged a bit against her desk and looked like she may fall into her seat. Instead, she lowered herself gently and pressed her manicured nails to her mouth, deep in thought.

"Well, maybe... Yeah, that could work. He's just so particular about when he gets it, and I don't have time to—"

"I completely get it. I'm happy to help."

Olivia nodded, slowly at first and then faster. Then she

ripped off a post-it note from her stack and scrawled Luke's order down, even going so far as to include the foam ratio and the temperature he liked it brewed at.

"Go to the shop on the corner and come right back. Remember to knock before you go in and be polite. He's busy today and bound to be irritable, so best not to make conversation. If he gives you trouble, just tell him I sent you."

"Alright," I said with a nod, then bounded off towards the door. I remembered to drop the sales sheet in the CFO's box and snatched up my purse before heading to the elevator. Sprinting most of the way down the congested city street, I ordered as quickly as I could and ferried the precious cargo back across the street and up the thirteen stories to the SkyBlue offices. I repeated a little mantra to myself in the elevator that everything was going to be fine and that I was going to make a much better second impression. Unfortunately, I was so focused on my little pep talk that I forgot to knock and shouldered open the door to Luke's office without warning. I caught Olivia's horrified expression as the door swung closed behind me, but by then, it was already too late.

The scene was nothing like I expected. Somehow, I had imagined that Luke would be sitting at his desk busily at work, or maybe standing with his back to me admiring the skyline from his corner office window. Instead, he was sitting in one of the cushy leather guest chairs arranged in a semi-circle off to the side of his office, and he wasn't alone.

There was a woman here with him, tall and dark-haired with stately high cheekbones. She was older than me but looked to be still in her twenties and wore a thick blue floral lace dress over a white slip. She looked surprised, but Luke, who sat beside a little boy of about seven or eight, merely raised an eyebrow at me.

"Oh God," I breathed. "Sorry! I should have knocked, so sorry. I'll just..."

"There's no use apologizing for something you've already done," Luke said, voice mellow and smooth despite his biting words. "If you're here, you may as well serve me my coffee."

With that, he turned back to the woman and the little boy as though nothing had happened, and gestured vaguely to a sleek end table near where he sat. I stood frozen for a moment, unable to read the woman. The woman's grey eyes were fixed on mine, but a moment later, she turned her attention back to Luke like I wasn't even there. Was this his wife? His child? I hadn't read anything online about him having a family. A rush of embarrassment flooded me at the memory of spending a solid half hour the night before scrolling through pictures of him, and I wanted nothing more than to duck out of the room and hide under the desk until he forgot I even worked there.

But leaving abruptly would be just as bad as arriving unannounced, and I had promised Olivia to do this job right, so I tentatively took a step forward.

The little boy was the only one who hadn't broken stride when I arrived and was still regaling Luke with stories of his friends at school, who by the sound of things were very excited about trading some sort of little trinket tied into his favorite TV show. Luke listened to him intently, smiling with a gentleness that I hadn't seen in any of his pictures, and I felt like I was witnessing something private, something no one outside this family was generally privy too.

To my great surprise, Luke carried on his conversation with the woman and the little boy as though I wasn't even there, hardly glancing up at me.

"I've told you I'm doing my best to get along with him," Luke said. "But I wouldn't get your hopes up."

"What about forgiveness?" The elegant woman asked, looking all the more put-together for her simmering anger.

"What about it?"

"He's family."

"He's your family, Sarah, and only mine by extension. I'll thank you to remember that the next time you come in here to try to guilt me into something."

"I'm not trying to guilt you into anything! I just asked you to come to dinner, to just spend a bit more time with us outside of work."

"Yes, you are; you just did it again."

I was painfully aware that this was not a conversation I was meant to overhear, no matter how calmly Luke spoke, or how lovingly he tousled the little boy's hair while he did it. This was a family dispute, and a messy one by the sound of things. I crossed the carpet to the three of them with my face burning. Was this some sort of punishment for interrupting? Or did Luke really care so little about a coffee-serving intern that he didn't see a reason to pause his conversation?

I was immensely grateful that there were no saucers or pot to fumble in this situation, and that "serving" coffee meant just setting Luke's to-go cup down where he indicated he wanted it. He glanced over to me only for a moment as he reached out to take it.

"What's happened to Olivia?"

"Um." My voice sounded so thin in my ears, tiny as a mouse. "She was in the middle of something. Didn't want you to miss your coffee."

"Send her in after you. Thank you, Emily."

I took this as my cue to leave and began immediately backing away. It took me a moment to register that he had said my name, and the sound burned in my ears. Had I told him my name in the elevator? No way. How had he learned it? Had he gone through all of his intern's files with a fine-tooth comb and taken the time to learn all of our names? That seemed very unlike the Luke Thorpe of media write-ups, or the one I had briefly encountered at this job. I felt confused and disoriented like I had taken one too many drinks at a New Year's Eve party, and suddenly wanted to lay my head down on something and close my eyes. I settled for scurrying out of the room and closing the door as quietly as possible behind me.

"What did you do?" Olivia hissed at me from her desk.

"I'm sorry!"

"God Emily, he hates that, you can't just——"

"I know, I know," I moaned, cringing inside and out. "I'm so sorry. But he wants to see you."

"Now?"

"I think so."

Olivia swore again, louder this time, and stood up. She ran her fingers through her hair once before approaching his door and made a show of knocking three times. The door was opened moments later, but not by Luke. Instead, the woman in the blue dress breezed quickly past Olivia, ushering her little boy forward. Her mouth was tight, and her face was red, as though she was trying to keep from crying or screaming. I couldn't meet her eyes as she moved past my desk in a gust of soft floral perfume, and it was almost a full minute later when I could pull together the courage to look back over to Luke's office. Olivia was still standing outside, looking pale. She waited for his inviting voice before pressing her way inside and shot me a death glare as she disappeared into his office.

I wished I had a nice hole to crawl into.

I sank down at my desk feeling numb and lightheaded, wishing with all of my might that there was some way to go back and undo the last ten minutes. I tried to turn back to my email and get some work done, but the tiny letters on the screen swam together until I felt nauseous. I wanted to put my head down on the desk and close my eyes, or lock myself in a bathroom stall and cry, but I was terrified that Olivia would come back outside and find me slacking off. I didn't see a way through this that didn't end with Olivia shouting my ear off, or worse, with me carrying the few personal possessions on my desk in a cardboard box down to the subway.

"I need this job," I muttered into the fingers that were pressed against my mouth. "God, please don't let me lose this job..."

A few agonizing moments later, Luke's door swung open, and I tried not to jump in my chair when Olivia strode stiffly over to me. Her brows were pulled tight in an expression I couldn't place, and I realized with some shock as she drew closer that it was concern. There was still anger there, and weary nerves from a work week she would be feeling all weekend, but there was genuine worry there as well.

"Olivia," I began in a small voice.

She shook her head, wringing her hands, and my voice dried up in my throat.

"He wants to see you."

"What?"

"Luke.... Mr. Thorpe wants to speak with you privately."

I blinked at her, my knuckles white where they gripped the

edge of my desk. Olivia lowered her voice, sounding a little threatening.

"Now, Emily."

I scrambled to my feet, reaching for my purse and then shaking my head at myself when I realized I wouldn't need it. I circled my cubicle tightly, smoothing my hair and desperately swiping on another coat of tinted lip balm as though it would save me from the worst of Thorpe's chastisement. I was sure my career was over. There was no way I was getting out of this in one piece.

I fell into step behind Olivia as she led me towards Luke's office, my face a white as a sheet.

"What did you say to him?" She asked.

"Nothing! I just served the coffee like he asked. I tried to apologize but—"

"He was asking all these questions about you. Where you go to school, how long you've worked here, things like that. I don't know what you did in there, but he's never taken an interest in any of the interns after they're hired. For God's sake, be on your best behavior. I've got no idea what he wants with you."

I fell silent for the rest of the walk, fighting off the dizziness swirling around in my skull. Olivia's bafflement was worse than anger. The anger I could handle; it would make sense under the circumstances. But the fact that she had no idea what our boss was thinking or what he wanted with me did not seem to bode well.

Olivia lingered by the door for a moment, listening. Then she knocked gravely and nodded to me once Luke's muted voice ordered me in.

Stepping into the office the first time had been a nerve-tingling experience, this time, it was heart-pounding. The room seemed much larger without the woman and child in it, but somehow Luke seemed even closer to me as he stood leaning against his desk facing me, hands tucked into his pockets, eyes boring a hole into my skull.

"Mr. Thorpe—" I began, my voice threatening to break. I thought I might cry. Or worse, blurt out the messiest, most over the top apology that came into my mind.

"Emily," He said before I had the chance to do either. His voice made my name sound weighted and valuable, like a diamond necklace worth more money than I could imagine. Or at least I thought it did; maybe the stress had fried my brain. "Come in here, please."

I did as I was told, closing the door on Olivia and the outside world and the last hope of escape I had. Luke beckoned me over to him with a sort of nod, and I took a few wary steps closer, doing my best to hold my shoulders back and my chin up. I was a professional. Even if my behavior a few minutes ago didn't show it. It was the least I could do to act like one now.

For a long moment, a heavy silence fell between us. I could hear nothing but the too-loud sound of my breath scraping through my lungs and the distant clicking of an analog clock. Luke was watching me, taking me in with the same eyes that had appraised me in the elevator. He was looking at me the way he might a fine antique, puzzling out what it was made of, if its provenance was trustworthy and if it would hold up under pressure. I said nothing and somehow managed to look him in the face.

"You've been with us for about three months now, is that correct?" He asked.

The question threw me. No introduction, no angry lecture? I swallowed.

"Nearly. I started in early May."

"I assume you're enrolled in one of the local universities?"

My heart started pounding faster in my chest. Why did he want to know where I went to school? Was he going to call the job placement department in the work-study office and tell them what an awful hire I was, and that they should never match me with another internship again? Could he do that?

"I'm at NYU," I managed.

"Studying?"

"Photography. With a minor in communications."

He probably didn't need that last little tidbit, but I threw it out anyway, to make sure that he didn't think I was hiding anything from him. Luke inclined his head to one side, his scrutiny of me becoming somehow even more intense. Tiny drops of sweat formed in my hairline, and I wondered how long I could keep this up before my legs buckled underneath me.

"Photography," he said with a hum of intrigue. "That's interesting; I don't think we have anyone with that background on staff right now. At least not in this department. Can I ask you something, Emily?"

"Of course Sir," I managed, even though I wanted to say something more.

"Why did you take the intern position at SkyBlue? I've seen your resume. It doesn't seem to keep with your past work history, and as you've said, you're a photographer. Shouldn't you be spending your summer snapping candids on the subway and forcing your friends to pose for editorial shoots?"

I couldn't tell if I detected a snide edge to his voice or not, then decided that he was actually genuinely interested, not belittling my passion at all.

"I wanted something more official," I said, choosing my

words carefully. "I thought it would be important for me to get more office experience, and SkyBlue is such a well-respected company that when I saw the ad, I knew I had to apply."

I hoped I wasn't laying it on too thick. It wasn't a lie, not strictly speaking. But this seemed like the worst time imaginable to admit that I had chosen this job from a random list at the last-minute or let the CEO of the company know that I was angling for a personal recommendation letter. So I stretched the truth and watched his expression warily. He was harder to read than anyone I had ever met, and he wore a face of vague, unyielding displeasure.

"Would you be interested in working with me on a project?" Luke asked. He made it sound like a natural question, not like an abrupt statement that sent me reeling.

"Work? With you?"

"That's generally what people do at their jobs."

Luke straightened up, moving a few paces closer to me with a smooth, almost feline air. I couldn't decide if he looked predatory like this or comforting, but there was no denying that he was tall and handsome and getting closer to me. Suddenly I didn't know what to do with my hands, and I curled them and uncurled them at my sides.

"I'm not sure what sort of experience I have that would be useful to someone like you," I managed because I still couldn't believe my ears. Luke's eyes flicked over me, hitting the ground before crawling up my body again.

"I'm sure you could be very useful to me. It sounds like you've got a lot of versatile skills."

All the blood in my body rushed to my face, and to other parts that I wouldn't mention in polite company. I was sure he hadn't meant it that way, but somehow I was still affected, body and soul, by his insinuation. Would I like being useful to him? A sinful picture coalesced in my mind of him bending me over the desk behind us, pulling my hair away from my neck and telling me to show him how versatile I was. I shuddered, which he must have noticed. Still, he didn't say anything, just waited for my response.

"What kind of project?"

"Photography, obviously. I'm tired of all the media outlets and photographers-for-hire traipsing in and out of my office. If I had someone on staff to do the heavy lifting for press releases, that would save me a lot of headaches."

Oh, of course. This is what he had meant all along, just a professional opportunity. One I should be grateful for. So why was there a small, quiet sensation of disappointment sitting cold in my stomach?

"I think I'd be interested in that, yes."

Luke almost smiled at me, the fleeting upward curve of his mouth nearly imperceptible.

"Perfect. I'll call you with details."

I blinked a bit, eyelashes fluttering. At some point he drifted even closer and was now standing directly in front of me, looking down at me. If I wanted to, I could reach out and touch him, press my palm against his broad chest or touch the strands of silver sprouting at his temples.

"Alright. I'll wait for your call, then."

"You're free to go. Unless..."

"Yes?"

"You need anything else from me?"

My breath caught in my throat. Men didn't usually stand this close to me unless they had a mind to kiss me, and I found, to my utter devastation, that some part of me did want Luke

Thorpe to kiss me. Just a fleeting, illicit duck of his head and pressing of his mouth to mine, the pressure of warm desire that was sure to make me melt in his hands.

But I didn't do anything. I just stood there, staring up at him with my eyes flickering from his eyes to his mouth. Then I said.

"No, sir."

"Good. I'll be in contact soon."

I turned to leave but was stopped with my hand on the door by Luke's effortlessly commanding voice.

"Emily?"

"Yes?" I asked, glancing over my shoulder.

"Knock next time, please."

I barely managed a nod before I slipped out the door and back into a world where I could breathe and see straight. Olivia shot me a worried look from her desk near Luke's office, but I spared her the details. I didn't want her to get any more worked up than she already was.

"He just told me to knock next time," I said breezily, hoping my bright red cheeks didn't give me away. "And he wanted me to introduce myself. We haven't been able to meet yet."

Olivia's dark eyes narrowed at this.

"Mr. Thorpe doesn't talk to interns, not generally."

I shrugged.

"Maybe he's changing his policy."

Olivia peered keenly at me once more, then rolled her eyes and turned back to her work.

"Control freak," she said under her breath, probably about Luke. Then, more audibly, she said, "You got lucky this time. But please, be more careful in the future."

"I promise."

"Good. You're free to go back to whatever it was you were doing."

I went back to my desk but quickly lost all hope of slipping back into the rhythm of work. My mind was on Luke, on his steady, steely eyes and the way they had examined every inch of me mercilessly. I knew for sure I would be staring at my phone all night, all week if I had to until I got his promised phone call. As it turned out, I didn't have to wait long.

Chapter Seven

LUKE

I promised myself I would wait. Play it cool, do a little more research on Emily and her background, and think of a genuinely compelling project to invite her into before calling her up on the phone. I promised myself I wouldn't waste her time with idle chatter or lunge at the opportunity to hear her voice like a high school kid with unsupervised phone time. I knew what a delicate balance there was between employers and employees at SkyBlue and that blurring those lines or an indiscretion could disrupt the entire ecosystem of the office. Emily was in an especially precarious position as a young intern working for a job experience credit at a large competitive company, and I knew if office rumors started swirling around, it would harm her the most. I promised myself that I would premeditate any further moves towards Emily. I wouldn't insert myself into her space or reach out to her right away.

But as good as I was at keeping my word to investors and employees, I had never been good at keeping promises to myself, especially when they involved denying myself something that I wanted.

So as soon as I got home to my luxury condo and dumped my briefcase down on the kitchen island, I brought my phone out and texted Olivia to send me Emily's number. It wouldn't look too unseemly, a boss asking for an employee's contact information. People did this sort of thing all the time. Olivia didn't have to know my reasons for wanting to keep a closer eye on Emily, only that I had a vested interest in one of my intern's professional development.

Surprisingly, I got pushback.

Why? She texted back promptly.

She will be taking on some new responsibilities in addition to her usual duties under Sonia. I want to be able to reach her directly if need be. I thought for a moment and then added, *For photo shoots,* hoping this would satisfy Oliva's curiosity.

I'm not sure if I'm allowed. You'll have to ask Sonia.

This is a time-sensitive thing, Olivia. Please do it.

There was silence for a moment, and I wondered if I had offended her so much that she was putting me on radio silence. I still didn't know where we stood after our little falling out a few days ago, although she accepted the peace offering I had asked one of the interns to deliver to her desk. Olivia was a hard nut to crack, as stubborn as she was smart, and you couldn't get her to do anything she hadn't already decided to.

But then, a few minutes later, she texted over Emily's number with no message attached. Good old Olivia. I could always rely on her.

Without waiting another moment, I selected Emily's number and hit call.

While the phone rang, I picked out a bottle of full-bodied

red wine from the wooden rack in my kitchen and poured myself a glass. I swirled the ruby liquid around while the electronic buzzing continued until I reached her answering machine. I quickly hung up, because while calling her home after hours was something I was comfortable doing, leaving a voice message seemed like a step too far.

Leave it alone, I urged myself. *She's not biting, so let her go.* There are other women.

But Emily was the only woman I had been able to think about for the past two months. Those huge blue eyes and that fiery silken hair and those slim, perfect hips had haunted my waking and sleeping hours ever since I had seen her on the street. I tried to forget. I tried to see other people and then barring that I tried to be patient with her when she dodged me at work. Eventually, something had to give. Apparently, that something was me.

I picked up the phone and dialed her again, chewing the inside of my lip while I waited for her to answer. The fumes from my wine were fragrant and ripe, smelling like dark soil and plums. I took a sip while I fidgeted in expectation. Then, after the phone rang three times, Emily picked up.

"Hello?"

She sounded a little skeptical, and I realized that I had never given her my private number so she would have no idea who to expect.

"Emily," I said, trying to keep the fondness out of my voice to keep this professional. "It's Luke Thorpe."

I hadn't given her explicit permission to use my first name but hoped that she would take the hint and slide into this new level of intimacy with me. We were going to be working very closely together, after all, one way or another.

"Oh!" She sounded a little startled. "Hello! I wasn't expecting to hear from you—"

"So soon, I know. But I thought it would be best to get the ball rolling as soon as possible. How are you?"

The segue from business to personal was abrupt, I knew, and I winced a little as I took another sip of my wine, but Emily didn't seem to care.

"Oh, I'm fine. Thank you!"

"Good good. Listen, I was thinking you and I might be able to work together on a photography project tomorrow morning."

"Oh! Uh, wow, that would be great. Definitely. Do you want me to bring over my equipment, or?"

"Yes, but feel free to keep it as simple as you like. We won't be doing a huge editorial shoot or anything like that. I would like us to get a sense of the space together and of each other. As photographer and subject," I added quickly, not wanting to hint at impropriety. As thrilled as I was about being alone with Emily, I wouldn't force anything she didn't want, and I didn't want her to feel uncomfortable coming to my office for a private photography session.

"That sounds perfect. When do you want me?"

It took every ounce of restraint in my body to not say "all the time." Instead, I said,

"6 am tomorrow. Sharp, I shouldn't have to add. I don't like tardiness."

"Of course," she said, in that eager, breathy way that drove me mad without her even trying.

"I'll warn you this probably won't be a very easy job," I said, a little more gently. "I've been told I'm an obstinate subject to photograph. I move around a lot and have all sorts of opinions."

Emily laughed on the other end of the phone. It was a crystalline, clear sound, so musical I could hardly believe she was just a college girl and not some old Hollywood starlet giving her best performance.

"I'll bet you're not as bad as some kids I photographed with the Easter Bunny at the mall last year. You haven't seen chaos until you've seen that."

This brought a smile to my lips. It felt good, to have her voice pressed against my ear in the privacy of my dim kitchen. I wondered where she was on the other end, if she was standing somewhere in her apartment or lounging in bed. Fleeting thoughts of Emily scantily clad cooling herself off in front of a fan or soaking in a bubble bath with her hair twisted up flashed through my mind. I tried to press them down, as mouth-watering as they were. I had to keep this as professional as possible, even if I was using my leverage as Emily's boss to get closer to her. Closer to her did not mean on top of her. Not unless she wanted that or any other position she might prefer.

"I'm sure I haven't. I'm happy you're on board with trying something new, Emily. I'll look forward to seeing you tomorrow morning."

"Same here! Thank you for the opportunity, uh..." She fumbled over my name, and I smiled.

"Luke. I'm not very formal with employees I work closely with."

"Luke, got it," she said, and I'm sure my voice had never sounded better coming out of a beautiful woman's mouth. "I'll see you tomorrow. Goodnight."

"Goodnight, Emily."

Our call disconnected with a quiet click, and it left me in stunned silence in my kitchen. I couldn't remember the last time I had gotten so worked up over someone. She barely had to do anything other than exist, and I was in knots, unable to sit still until I saw her again or spoke to her.

Her ghost seemed to follow me through the halls of my apartment as I wrapped up my workday and flipped on the hot water in my shower. Everything, from the smell of her perfume to the way her lips curved into a nervous smile slipped in and out of my thoughts, intoxicating me entirely.

When I stepped into the shower, and the water hit my back, I almost felt as though her arms were encircling me from behind, as though her lips were pressing light kisses between my shoulder blades. It was so easy to imagine her hands traveling over my stomach, past my navel, and lower and lower, until...

I groaned and flipped the shower onto a cold setting, shuddering as reality hit me in an icy burst. What on earth had I gotten myself into here?

Chapter Eight

EMILY

here was almost nothing that could get me excited about hauling my half-conscious body out of bed at the crack of dawn, but I woke up on the day of my photography session with SkyBlue's CEO feeling rested, electric even. I laid out my camera and outfit the night before, which had taken a very long time. As I deliberated between heels or flats, a red dress or a green one, I wondered why I cared so much. My stomach was doing somersaults like I was getting ready for a first date, not a photography session. I had done plenty of these before, with smiling toddlers and newly engaged couples and high school graduates. So what was different here?

Luke. Luke Thorpe was different.

I tried not to think about the way he made me feel while I applied my lipstick. Tried to ignore the way every nerve in my body stood at attention when he looked at me or the way the sound of his voice over the phone had sent a pleasant little shudder through me the night before. This was business, the important kind. I had to keep it professional, but it was so hard not to let my mind wander when he spoke in that commanding tone.

I tried to put the inappropriate thoughts out of my mind as I made the brisk 5 am walk to my subway station, but it proved difficult. Thoughts of Luke's breath on my neck invaded my mind while I fumbled through my purse for my metro card, and I could almost feel him sliding his hands through my hair as I rocked along with the underground rhythm of the subway. This would not work. If I couldn't keep it together for this fantastic opportunity, there was no way I was making it through this summer job, much less make it to Paris.

I almost darted from the subway stop exit across from SkyBlue straight into the office, but then I glanced down at my watch and realized I still had twenty-five minutes. My eyes drifted to the coffee shop on the corner where I had been sent by Olivia the day before. If I hurried, I could bring Luke his coffee order and still make it to our meeting with time to spare.

So, twelve minutes later I was riding the elevator up to Luke's office with my camera bag slung over my shoulder and a custom espresso in my hands, trying not to sweat through my thin blouse. Luke hadn't been lying about us getting an early start. No one else, not even the most over-eager office climbers, were at their desks at not-quite six in the morning. I stifled a yawn as I waited outside his door, then knocked three times, as I had seen Olivia do.

"Come in," Luke said, and my heart fluttered.

I pressed in with what I hoped was a bright and winning smile and carefully closed the door behind me. Luke was seated at his desk, looking as severe and intimidating as always in a finely cut slim grey suit, his hair swept back from his face. There weren't any papers on his desk, and his computer monitor displayed a screensaver, no email or sales reports. Had he just been waiting for me to arrive? I wasn't late, was I?

Nerves flooded my system, knocking down any reckless confidence I had talked myself into on the elevator ride up.

"Good morning," I said as brightly as I could, moving across the room to him.

"Good morning," he replied levelly, taking me in with an arched brow. I adjusted the camera bag on my shoulder, hoping he wasn't regretting his decision to let me photograph him after he saw how small my equipment bag was. The camera had been a gift from my father before he died, and though I treasured it, I knew the trusty Nikon I learned to shoot on was outmoded and hadn't been professional grade, to begin with. Still, I had got a lot of use out of it over the years, and I hoped the results would banish any doubts Luke was having now.

"Sleep well?" I asked, as I set down the equipment bag on the side table near the cluster of chairs and unpacked my lenses. It sounded forced and awkward coming out of my mouth, especially since I wasn't in the habit of discussing personal things with the boss I had only met yesterday, but I knew that making conversation was key. You had to put the client at ease and make them feel like they weren't being arranged and studied. They needed to forget they were being photographed. This was the part of the job that required the most finesse, and a skill most hobbyists never developed.

"No, actually," he said thoughtfully. I could feel his eyes on my back, warm and heavy, and I was grateful that he couldn't see the flush that was crawling up my chest and peeking out of my neckline.

"Bad dreams?"

"Not bad. I was just restless."

"That's a shame," I said lightly, knowing that I probably shouldn't pry anymore. This uncharted territory between Luke and I was unsteady. Did we have some kind of personal relationship now, the kind he had with Olivia? Or did he invite employees in before office hours for personal projects with no intention of getting to know them better? With Luke Thorpe, it was hard to say.

I turned back towards him, slotting a lens onto my camera. I didn't know where to look. Looking him straight in the face was sure to make my heart pound, but I had to look at him to photograph him properly.

"So, um... What sort of photographs did you have in mind?"

"Nothing special. If we could get a couple of shots of me in the office to have on hand when someone asks for a press release, it would save me a lot of headache in the future. It doesn't have to be anything too creative, just professional."

I had suspected something like this but hoped he would come prepared with more specifics. A shoot in which I had free range was exciting; it gave me almost unlimited options. But it was also terrifying because, well... I had unlimited options. All the power was in my hands. The choices mine to make about how I wanted him positioned, lit, and captured by my camera.

My hands started to sweat around my Nikon.

"I'd like to do a couple of test shots first," I said, trying to sound confident. "If that's alright."

"By all means. I'm at your disposal."

I swallowed hard. He hadn't moved at all and was still seated at his desk, looking like one of those beautiful busts of Roman emperors they had at the Met, but in a suit. His bearing had the strange ability to unsettle me and put me at ease at the same time. I felt like I had known him for much longer than the few minutes we shared in the elevator and his office. But that was impossible, wasn't it? I hadn't met Luke before last week. Maybe it was all the editorial shoots I had seen of his square-jawed profile gazing out into the middle distance.

I snapped a few experimental photographs of him at his desk, experimenting with the lighting and color balance until I remembered the peace offering I had almost forgotten. I quickly plucked up the still-hot cup of coffee and set it on the edge of Luke's desk. In addition to giving him something to drink while I adjusted my settings between photographs, I thought the branded paper cup from a local chain gave the office a lived-in, authentic feeling. It would make the pictures look like a true slice-of-life like I had caught him in the middle of an average morning.

Luke glanced down at the coffee cup, his dark eyebrows drawing together slightly.

"What's that?"

"It's your espresso order. I picked it up on the way into work this morning, and I thought it might be—"

"I didn't ask for it."

His voice was flat, more confused than angry, but I could tell I had displeased him. I stood awkwardly with the camera between my hands, looking at the coffee and then him. I knew that he had a reputation for being particular, but this seemed a little ridiculous. I was at his office at six in the morning, and I brought him coffee out of the goodness of my heart. Even if he didn't want it, I felt like a simple thank you was in order.

"Um," I said, trying to keep my voice level and polite. "I know, but it's early, and I thought you might want a cup of coffee for our session. These things can be long and boring."

"I don't have my espresso until the afternoon," he said, and plucked up the cup without another word and discarded it into the waste bin near his desk. I felt like the cup dropped with a heavy thud into my stomach instead of the trash can, and my face flushed in anger. Genius CEO or not, that was a spoiled, petty thing to do.

"Alright, fine," I muttered, seething to myself as I looked back down at my camera. It had broken my concentration, and I couldn't remember what settings I already altered.

"Sorry, have I upset you?" Luke asked. I glanced up to him in disbelief. He rose from his seat and was leaning against the desk lazily now, the way he had been when he had called me back into his office yesterday. His presence filled the room.

I knew I should bite back my irritation and insist that everything was fine, that nothing was wrong. But despite how grateful I was for this opportunity, Luke Thorpe had been playing my nerves like violin strings for days now, and I was getting sick and tired of it. I couldn't read him, couldn't anticipate his movements, and certainly couldn't predict what he would do or say next. He was probably like this with everyone, but I didn't appreciate his erratic behavior.

"That's sort of wasteful, don't you think?"

Luke quirked an eyebrow at me. "I don't really care about waste."

"I see."

I turned back to my camera, willing myself to shut up and get on with the shoot before I got myself fired. But Luke wasn't done with me yet. He straightened and took a few steps closer, out of my frame and into my personal space.

"If you can't handle the stress of this job, I'm happy to find someone else who can. There's no shame in not being up to something, just say the word, and I won't waste any more of your time."

Anger rose in my throat.

"I want this position, and I'm prepared for it."

"Are you sure?"

"I will not beg if that's where you're going. Listen, I'm happy to run errands and make copies and take pictures and do anything else that you want, but you have to work with me for this whole project to work. If you're going to be condescending, I'm going to get hurt, and I don't think I need to apologize for that."

I could barely believe the words flying out of my mouth, but my thinned patience had snapped under the strain of too many hours on the subway, too many new tasks at work, and not enough sleep. I knew I was just an intern, but I felt like I deserved a little respect.

Emotions I couldn't name flashed behind Luke's eyes, too fast for me to pin down. He was standing very close to me now, and I realized I must have drifted closer to him during my angry diatribe. His eyes were green, very green, with tiny flecks of black that seemed so familiar to me; it made a chill run down my spine.

"I don't think this is going to work," he said, voice sounding a little tight. "Thank you for your time, Emily, and your willingness to take on another project. I realize I've asked too much of you, and you're welcome to resume your normal workday duties."

"What? Why? I didn't say I couldn't do this, I know my abilities and I think this is a good idea for both of us so why won't you let me—"

"This isn't a conversation."

"It is now. You're pushing me," I said, something close to a threat rising in my voice as I stared him down, cheeks on fire.

"I am," he said. His eyes were dark, hungry, pinning me in place. The air felt scorching hot despite the AC unit whirring in the corner.

"Why?"

"To see what you'll do."

His words rung in my ears, and my mouth felt dry. Before I knew what I was doing, I was closing the gap between us. My body moving faster than my mind could process, heat tingling inside every part of me. This was forbidden, but anger and desire were swirling around together in my chest so powerfully that I thought I would burst if I didn't do anything about it.

I tilted my face up into his defiantly, and before I had an opportunity to do or say anything else, Luke Thorpe caught my face in his hands and kissed me.

The pressure was intense, the sudden warmth of him and scrape of his stubble against my cheek almost overpowering. He kissed me with such passionate intensity that I could hardly breathe. I clung to the shoulders of his suit jacket and tried to keep up with him, my head spinning. I could barely remember my own name, or that this man was my boss and we should certainly not be doing this. Certainly not on company time. Instead, I kissed him, making a little pleasured noise when his hand cupped my chin, and his tongue scorched against my own. This, I decided, was definitely worth getting fired for.

Suddenly Luke broke away, severing our kiss. He was still clutching me tightly, his fingers curled around my upper arms exposed by my short-sleeved dress, but he held me almost at arm's length. I was panting, and his face was a torrent of dark emotion.

"Emily," He said, and the rasp of desire in his voice flooded my body with arousal all over again.

"I," I began unsteadily. The room was spinning, but as it slowly came to a stop, a horrible feeling of cold regret took over. "Oh God. I... I'm sorry."

"Don't apologize; it's my fault."

His fault? Had he suspected something like this would happen? That didn't make any sense; I thought the overheated fantasies I had of Luke pressing me against elevator walls lived entirely in my mind.

"I'm your employer," he said, still strained. His mouth was flushed from being crushed against mine and was so tempting to look at that I had to tear my eyes away. "This is a breach of ethics; I can't——"

"I know," I said, nodding vigorously. Even though he was taking the blame, I somehow felt like I should be the one in trouble. But he didn't seem angry with me at all. "I know. It can never happen again. It won't. We were just both..."

"Stressed," he finished, in the voice of a man who was used to making executive decisions in crises. His hands disappeared from my arms and were now straightening his tie. "And sleep deprived."

"Right. Of course. Listen, I'm just going to gather up my things and get out of your hair..."

"There's no need for that now," Luke said with a chuckle. The sound was a low, warm rumble that made me want him even more. He seemed amused that I thought I could just run away and leave whatever electric moment had transpired between us behind like he knew better than I that there was no forgetting this. He leaned back against his desk, hip at an angle, suit fitting him even better somehow now that it was slightly askew. "You were right, I was pushing you earlier, but I want you on this project if you can handle it. I'm happy to get back to business if you are."

I sagged against the edge of one of the leather chairs, a safe distance away from Luke Thorpe and his smoldering green eyes.

"You mean... I'm not fired?"

"No, Emily, you're not fired. In fact..." Luke tilted his head and took me in again, making me feel stripped bare and searched. "I've got a press meeting in here at nine. Do you think you can have some sample photos ready by then, just to show on a computer?"

I nodded, still feeling dazed from his kiss as I retrieved my camera. Intrusive thoughts of his fingertips on my skin, his mouth on mine, wouldn't leave my head.

"I'm sure I could, yeah."

"Good." Luke gave me a smile that would have shamed the devil. "I think you and I are going to be working quite closely together."

Chapter Nine

LUKE

*E*ven though I was the object of observation, the subject being photographed by Emily's agile camera, I couldn't stop staring at her. I studied every inch of her like a piece of fine art, from the white curve of her throat to the gnawed nails on her long, red-knuckled fingers, to the way she pressed her tongue to the back of her front teeth when she was concentrating. Having an hour alone with her in my office, the silence broken only when Emily told me to turn my head into the light or adopt a different pose, was absolute bliss. Except, of course, for the way it was torture because I couldn't reach out and draw her back into me and kiss that beautiful red mouth all over again.

As much as I may have indulged in fantasies about Emily, the kiss hadn't been my intention. I had flirted with her, cajoled her, and prodded her when she bristled to understand what made her tick. I was probably just as taken aback as she was when she pressed herself up on her tiptoes in front of me, but I wasted no time in seizing the moment. If she was going to present herself for the taking, I was going to take her.

But that, of course, would be insane. Emily was still my employee and working for me on company time. Even more than that, she was nearly young enough to be my daughter. As much as I wanted to get her alone, to unravel the thoughts inside her head and watch her come undone under my hands, that wasn't possible.

At least, not right now.

Our photo session stretched on for nearly an hour, our little spat and indiscretion accounted for. By the time she was finished, I was sure she had adjusted me at least fifty times. Standing still for a photograph was surprisingly tiring, and I began to regret tossing the coffee Emily brought. I hadn't meant to be insulting, but I didn't see any use for it, and there were more important things going on than breakfast, so I discarded it the way I would anything that didn't serve me. But Emily seemed upset about not just the waste but of my disregard for her effort, for her. Her fiery spirit was even more enticing to me than the way her lashes shuttered her huge blue eyes when she was feeling shy. Keeping my hands to myself might prove a more challenging endeavor than I had expected.

"Well," Emily said, flipping through the last couple of shots on her digital camera. "I think I've got plenty to work with now. I'll do some basic editing and pull together five or six to show at the press meeting if you'd like."

"Perfect," I said. "Can you stay? Our in-house team will be here in twenty or so."

"Stay? You want me here for the meeting?"

"Of course," I said smoothly. "I'm not very well going to show off your work and not show you off as well."

This brought a little color into her cheeks, and I had to admit I loved having such a visceral effect on her. I wondered what else I could do to bring a flush of color to her face and her mouth.

Emily lowered herself gently onto the edge of a chair. She looked like she didn't know what to do with herself like she was scrambling for a way to show gratitude.

"It's really not any trouble," I continued, hoping that my words would smooth over the two little lines of concern that had gathered between her eyebrows.

"Thank you for the opportunity," she said at last. There was a sea of emotion swirling behind those blue eyes, deep enough that I could get lost and drown in them if I didn't watch my step. "I appreciate you bringing me on like this."

Her sincerity caught me off guard. I was used to people thanking me profusely for interviews or positions, and people telling me that working at SkyBlue had changed their life or launched their career. But Emily seemed so earnest, so tentative. I hadn't thought about how precarious things were for her, as a college student with no work experience trying to make a living in one of the toughest cities in the world. People in her position didn't get opportunities like this every day, and while I hadn't thought twice about involving a photographer in a high-level marketing meeting, it was the sort of experience most students would kill for.

"Of course," I said, and I was surprised at how soft my voice came out sounding. I rarely had much of time for emotions; mine or other people's. "You're very talented, and you come highly recommended by Olivia. The photographs you've shown me so far are good; you deserve to be here."

For a moment, I thought she might cry, and the urge to rush

over and wrap her up in my arms overtook me. I resisted, pulling my fingers into fists in my pockets with effort, but soon she was composed again.

"Great. I'm excited."

My press team arrived just on time, with representatives from the marketing and public relations department sitting at the ready to draft releases and brainstorm brand campaigns. While some CEOs only got involved with public-facing issues once other departments reached their consensus and brought materials over for review, I liked to meet with my team monthly to keep my fingers on the pulse of what was going on.

Emily lingered by the semicircle of chairs beside my desk, looking stiff and spooked as the team filed in. I could see that a bustling morning had already begun in the office. I could see the activity outside every time the door swung open, and a member of the press team entered. Oliva was already at her desk, on the phone with someone while she jotted notes down on a pad.

I shook hands with marketing and PR people and made the usual rounds of hellos and how are yous, then gestured over to Emily.

"This is Emily Greenwater. She's one of our newest hires from NYU, and she'll be working closely with me on some photography projects in the future. I asked her to sit in and show us some of the content she's got. We might be able to use it in the Dallas press releases."

Everyone smiled at her and murmured their introductions. Each of the seven or eight people gathered shook her hand. Anyone could see that she was young, probably too young to get a spot at a table like this. Since I had introduced her, she had automatic credibility in a room filled with industry veterans. Her smiles were nervous, and she had the tight body language of a teenage girl out on her first date, but she managed to be charming all the same as she sank into one of the leather chairs. I took the seat beside her, close enough to comfort her and far enough away that she wouldn't feel I was looming over her. I was also just far enough away that I couldn't easily touch her, which seemed like the safest bet under the circumstances.

"How are we coming along on the Dallas project?" I asked, getting the ball rolling on the morning's itinerary. These meetings tended to skew towards everyone talking over each other and bouncing ideas off each other, but we had ostensibly gathered to discuss the scheduled opening of a second SkyBlue location in Dallas next year. The company was growing at an exponential rate, demanding new offices and new manufacturers outside of New York City. Dallas had been an excellent decision both financially and geographically, but the good people of Texas still needed to be convinced that SkyBlue was a net good to Dallas so they would send their best and brightest to apply for our jobs.

"Early focus groups show that it's important to people in our target demographic to feel as though they have some kind of personal connection to a company," one of my best market behaviorists said. She was sitting in a clump with many of my other guests at the end of a rectangular glass table, flipping through graphs. "People want to feel like the corporation they get their car from has a real human face."

"Me," I said.

"That's right," one of the higher-ups from PR said. "You've been getting a lot of amazing press about your financial profile and work on SkyBlue, and more local outlets have done more personal explorations of your life as well, but Dallas will want to get to know the man behind the company a bit before opening their arms to you. We were thinking maybe a flyby tour of the city? You wouldn't have to stay long, shake some hands, meet with some local business owners, be seen eating at some local joints."

"That's not a bad idea, but I just can't swing travel right now, not with the launch bearing down on us. Scratch that."

"What about another photoshoot?" Another public relations expert asked. "We could do something personable, really naturalistic. Maybe include photos with a signed personal letter to the people of Dallas."

"That's more like what I was thinking." I glanced over to Emily, indicating with my eyes that I would be talking about her soon. She remained silent and rapt throughout the entire conversation, sometimes taking notes on a little pink pad she pulled out of her purse. "We were actually experimenting with some test shots. I think they'll give you a sense of what I'd like to see in the new press releases."

The head of advertising took off her wire-rim glasses and set them down on the table, nodding to me with a jut of her chin. She was a severely editorial looking woman immaculately dressed in white and navy, and Emily had been hazarding terrified glances in her direction ever since we sat down.

"Let's see them. You have prints?"

She was speaking to Emily now, not to me, and I kept silent to give my newly ascended intern room to speak. For a second I thought she would clam up and choke, but then she retrieved her laptop and pulled up a couple of the photos she had selected as examples and done a quick editing pass on in the ten minutes or so we had between the photo shoot and the press meeting.

"No, but I've got a few test shots."

She took the computer from Emily and studied the

photographs hard for a moment. One of her assistants glanced over her shoulder, raising her eyebrows.

"You took these?" The head of advertising asked, looking over to the both of us. Emily looked a little pale, but she nodded and said,

"Just this morning."

I was proud of her. It was good that she didn't minimize her work or let others take credit for what she had done.

"These are good," the older woman pronounced. "You've got a great eye for light. You even made Luke look like he wasn't in a terrible mood when you took them, so well done in that regard."

There was a smattering of light laughter, and Emily smiled as well, but I saw that there was more than levity behind her eyes. She was profoundly affected by the compliment. I wondered how many other professionals had even seen her work, much less complimented its composition. I had never been an artist of any kind, but I knew New York City could be brutal to artists, who had to beg, borrow, and burn themselves out to get any recognition.

Underneath the table, I reached out and lightly squeezed Emily's bare knee. It was a fleeting touch, one that I hoped didn't come across as too unprofessional considering the circumstances. I wanted her to know that I was proud of her, that she was worth all the acclaim.

Emily's leg jolted underneath the table, and her eyes flicked to me in surprise. They were practically glowing with warm radiance, and I found, to my dismay, that I wanted to kiss her just as badly as I had an hour ago when she was staring me down defiantly, her camera in her hands.

Now I withdrew my hand to my lap where it couldn't wander and cause any more trouble. The marketing meeting continued around us, with members of my team sipping their coffees and discussing what the best way to introduce SkyBlue to the people of Dallas was. They wanted the company to make the right impression as it opened up its second headquarters in Texas, and they wanted it to feel like an integrated part of the local cityscape as soon as possible.

The meeting flowed naturally from there, and to my delight, Emily even took part in some of the conversations, tentatively at first but then with increasing enthusiasm. She had the good sense not to comment on things she knew nothing about and to ask questions when she didn't understand something, which I appreciated immensely. She didn't seem to consider herself either a stupid person or one who was too good to learn anything new.

Eventually, a press release and personal letter were decided on that would feature one of the photographs Emily had captured of me. It was a far cry from any of the pictures that were usually seen of me in the press. Instead of positioning me in a traditional stance of power, Emily had instructed me to hold my body comfortably, and she had snapped a photo of me when I was laughing at something she said to me. In the photo, I was leaning against my desk, one hand adjusting the cufflinks on a sleeve while I smiled with genuine amusement. My eyes, I knew, were fixed just out of frame on Emily's face. I still looked powerful but radiated a friendlier, man-of-the-house air, not like I was getting ready to go bring down a competitor. I had only been to Dallas once and was staggered by how often people smiled, greeted each other, and talked to absolute strangers. They would probably appreciate this picture.

After a game plan had been decided on, everyone stood, straightened their skirts and slacks, and tossed out their empty coffee cups before milling around the room. A few people stopped to chat with Emily before they made for the door, and her face lit up when they asked about her photography studies or how long she worked for SkyBlue. I couldn't help but watch out of the corner of my eye, even as I shook hands with colleagues. She was radiant in every way, and I was filled with a ferocious pride to see her win the appreciation of jaded old advertising execs. There was certainly more to her than met the eye, and the eye had plenty to work with.

A few minutes later, we were finally alone again, just Emily and I. The voices of the press team faded down the hallways as I watched her tangle and untangle her fingers nervously. She didn't know whether she could go. Or maybe she didn't want to. Was she reluctant to leave the private world we had formed together in the early morning hours?

"You were wonderful," I said.

Emily hooked a long strand of fiery hair behind her ear, smiling shyly. She was incandescent when she smiled; it made her eyes catch the light and gleam.

"I didn't really do anything."

"Yes, you did," I insisted. My voice was low, careful not to be overheard by Olivia sitting at her desk outside. What was I afraid of? I was just an employer complimenting his employee on a job well done, wasn't I? So why did I feel like there was indiscretion in the air like something was going on that shouldn't be revealed to the outside world? "I threw you in with people way out of your paygrade, and you were poised and articulate. Your photographs deserve the praise they got."

"Thank you," she said softly. She was standing so close to me with one hand crossed over her chest, gripping her upper arm. She looked so vulnerable, half-hugging herself in the big, empty office like she had the night the carjackers had left her rattled. I ached to take her into my arms, to show her in every way imaginable that she was worthy. I wanted her to feel safe, and I wanted her to open herself up to me.

"Of course."

I moved closer to her against my will; I couldn't stand to be so far from her. I gently cupped her cheek in my hand, fingers disappearing into her curtain of red hair, and her eyes flickered up to mine in soft surprise. Why was it so hard to keep my hands off her, even though I promised myself I would? Emily made a soft sighing sound and shifted closer me, and before I knew what was happening, her mouth was warm and insistent on mine.

I cupped her face in both hands, losing myself in her warmth and her sugared white floral perfume. Her body against mine was soft and supple, pressing in with delicious heat as I deepened the kiss, drowning in the taste of her. Her small hands roamed across my chest, sending electricity coursing through my body. When she moaned my name, the sound vibrated over my lips and through my chest. I knew we were both fucked.

"Say that again," I said, my voice coming rough.

"Luke," she said. There was a little whine in her voice that sent a shudder through me, and I couldn't hold myself back anymore. I wrapped my arms around her waist and hoisted her slight frame up. Her legs latched around my waist as she gave herself over to me, chasing my kisses with her own urgency. I carried her to the corner of my desk and devoured her neck and collarbone with kisses while her fingers fumbled with the buttons on my shirt.

"I want you," I growled into her neck, as directly and with as much command as I showed towards everything else in my life. "I've wanted you since I met you."

Emily could hardly manage words since my fingers were now circling her secret hot center through her panties, but she nodded vigorously and pulled me in for another kiss. I knew that this was wrong, that I shouldn't be undressing my nineteen-year-old intern on my desk in the middle of the workday, but we were past the point of no return now. This wasn't going to be finished until we both were.

Chapter Ten

EMILY

*L*uke's kisses were punishing and tender in equal measure as his hands explored every inch of my body. I shuddered with delight when they trailed down my throat, or fondled my breasts, passing over my stomach before they dipped lower to tease me with a pleasure so intense that I almost cried. I knew I wanted Luke, I had also wanted him from the moment I saw him, but I hadn't realized how damn much until this moment. My body was already screaming for release as he kissed me towards oblivion, tongue circling my own as he hitched my skirt up around my hips.

I was kissing Luke Thorpe, THE Luke Thorpe. He was fondling me on his desk and tugging my panties down over my ankles. We were actually going to do this. Part of me knew that this was absolutely off-limits, was going to cause unimaginable trouble for both of us, and maybe jeopardize our careers. But I couldn't bring myself to care, not with this need coursing through my body and Luke half dressed in front of me. I was going to pay for this, I knew, but I was clay in his hands, eager to be worked and molded into whatever shape he desired.

Luke gasped when I wrapped my fingers around his hard length, and I grinned against his mouth, pleased with myself. I pumped him in my hand as he freed my breasts from my dress; it would probably be ruined after this. I cried out when his fingers circled my nipple, painfully erect, and he pulled me tight against him.

He sank his teeth into my neck when he entered me, just hard enough to make me gasp, and I dug my fingernails into his back. I freed him from his restrictive suit jacket and could feel his powerful muscles moving beneath the thin fabric of his button-down shirt as he set a steady pace. My legs were quivering around him as he worked me mercilessly, pushing me further and further over the edge. I moaned when he groaned my name, and a few of his fingers came up to press against my swollen mouth, reminding me of the crowds of people sitting at their desks on the other side of the thin wall. I took his fingers into my mouth, delirious with desire, and sucked them while he drove into me.

Luke's fingers dug into my hips, pulling me as close to him as our bodies would fit as he thrust in and out of me. The slight pain of his fingernails digging into my skin was intoxicating, and I cried out his name as I threaded my fingers through his hair. The world was a blur of pleasure, and his breath was hot and labored in my ear. I was so close to earth-shattering release, and I could feel his cock twitching inside me. We were both so close, so close to—

"Luke?"

The voice was hesitant, neither of ours and worst of all, coming from inside the room. I threw my head up from Luke's shoulder just in time to see Oliva press her way through the door and drop her notebook in shock. She swore and threw her hand over her mouth, and I gasped and tried to wriggle out from under Luke, but it was too late. She had seen. Everything.

"Luke," she hissed, slamming the door behind her and stepping into the room.

Luke had, by this point, realized we were not alone and was scrambling to right his appearance and cover me up the best he could. I wanted to cry when he pulled out of me, leaving me with nothing but the memory of how good it felt to be full of him and on the brink of climax.

"Olivia—"

"I cannot believe you," she began, hissing the words through her teeth. I had seen Olivia stressed before, but never this honest-to-God furious. "Are you insane? I've seen wild behavior from your before, but this is really something else. This is grade A son-of-a-bitch right here."

A purplish color was rising in her dark cheeks, and her eyes were aflame with anger.

Directed toward Luke, I realized. Not towards me. In that instant, it was like I didn't even exist, like Luke had gotten himself into this mess entirely by himself without my willing aid. I expected Olivia to be too embarrassed to talk to either of us or to throw her hands over her eyes and shuffle out of the room, but she stood there and stared Luke down like she had every right to, like she was a member of his family who came to read him his rights.

"Olivia," he huffed again, tucking in his shirttail. His hair was beyond saving, askew from my fingers running through it. Nudity aside, there was no question about what we had just been doing. "Would you please just let me explain?"

"What's there to explain Luke? You've got the intern spread like a buffet on your desk during office hours. I cannot believe you. I thought you were better than this. I really did."

"Olivia," he snapped. "Listen to me. This... was not planned. This was not supposed to happen; I'm not having some kind of affair under your nose. Emily and I... she was helping me on a project and we—"

"Oh, really?" Olivia asked, arching an eyebrow. She cast a disparaging glance down to Luke's crotch. "Your 'project,' huh?"

Sensation was returning to my body in dull waves as the shock wore off. I hastily tugged my dress down over my hips and righted my neckline. I wiped a hand over my mouth even though I knew that Luke had kissed off any of the lipstick he had smeared.

"We got carried away in the heat of the moment. For God's sake, these things happen, we're all just humans. You and I did stupid shit when we were in college, didn't we? You've come to me with so many crazy stories about the guys you were seeing—"

"Yes, exactly, you just said it, in college! You're a grown-ass man, and that girl is barely legal. Employee or not, that is fucked up."

"Do I get to have a say in any of this?" I asked, my voice hoarse and thin. After all the day's excitement, I felt like I might slip off the edge of Luke's desk and hit the floor if I wasn't careful. He seemed to sense this and put a steadying hand on my knee. Olivia didn't look so sympathetic.

"If I were you, I wouldn't want any part in whatever this is, Emily. Are you okay?"

"Yes, I'm fine! He wasn't.... everything was consensual, okay?"

"I assumed that. It doesn't make this look any better. God,

Emily, you're a student intern... This is... This is bad, alright? You at least realize that this whole situation is bad?"

She was talking to me like I was a high schooler caught with her skirt up, bent over her teacher's desk, and I resented her for it.

"I might be stupid, but I'm not a child. I know what we did, alright? Like Luke said we just got carried away. I think it's safe to say that this has been an emotional month for everyone with all the press about the new product launches." I felt ridiculous trying to talk business to Olivia with my lacy bra poking over my neckline and my makeup in shambles from Luke's punishing kisses, but I had lost my shame somewhere along the way. If she saw what she saw, we could talk frankly with one another.

"You aren't wrong, but that doesn't make it alright."

"I didn't say it did."

"Olivia," Luke said in that steely, confident tone that made him sound like he had everything under control, even though he had been about to come undone inside me minutes ago. "Come here."

Now Olivia looked truly scandalized.

"I'm not joining whatever club of bad choices you two have going on—"

"Don't be an idiot. I want you to sign something."

I was left sitting stunned on the edge of Luke's desk as he went rummaging through folders in a drawer in his desk, flipping through the labels without looking up to meet either of our eyes. I had no idea what was going on. Could he really be thinking of work at a time like this? Was he just going to breeze into asking Olivia to read off his weekly checklist and bring him his schedule as though nothing happened?

Luke slapped down a piece of photocopied paper on the

desk, then retrieved a heavy fountain pen and passed it across the table to Olivia. She drifted tentatively closer to us and was now standing right beside me. Somehow this made her presence in the room more real, and embarrassment seized me all over again.

"It's a nondisclosure form," my employer, my client, the man who I just let hoist me up onto his desk and strip off my panties, said.

Olivia shot a daggered glance at him.

"You're just gonna shut me up, Luke, is that it? After all we've been through? I've known you since you were a kid you ungrateful—"

"This isn't blackmail or hush money. It's just here to protect all of us, in case anything gets out."

The thought sent a whole new terror rushing through me. Get out? What could get out? Terrified visions of paparazzi snapping pictures outside his window or of disgruntled office workers hearing me beg for him through the walls danced through my head. My God. That could ruin me. Forget losing out on France. This could get me expelled since this was a school-sponsored internship. I was sure Luke, and I had just very thoroughly and enthusiastically shattered some NYU code of conduct bylaws.

Olivia was still glaring at him, but she picked up the pen.

"If I sign this, you promise me that this never happens again."

"Of course," Luke said, so sincerely that my heart hurt. His eyes darted over to me, green and searching, and I nodded.

"Yeah," I said once I had swallowed to free up my dry throat. "It's not going to happen again. We promise."

Olivia picked up the pen and then signed her name in one

defiant swoop. I was sure the fine print didn't have specific details about a boss hooking up with his employee in it, but Olivia had probably signed plenty of things like this before. Maybe Luke had even asked her to sign under similar circumstances before. The thought made me squirm with discomfort. Was I the first girl this had ever happened with?

"It's done," Olivia said. "Listen to me, both of you... I am willing to overlook this. I'm serious. I'm willing to chalk this up to a shit decision made during a shit month, and I'm willing to grant you that you're both overworked and probably needed to blow off a little steam, anyway. But I just... can't handle this, alright? Luke, for my sake, I can't field paparazzi calls about your intern I just..."

"I know. I know, Olivia, and I'm sorry. It won't happen again."

"Thank you," she said, looking tired. "Emily..."

Her voice trailed off, and she looked me over with those keen, dark eyes, unable to decide what to do with me. I was sure she had no shortage of things she'd like to say to me, but she weighed them before she spoke, and I thanked God for that. I felt like I could be pushed over the brink into tears at the drop of a hat.

"You're a smart girl," was all she said. "Act smart."

Olivia threw Luke one more cutting glance before she slipped out the door, and then it was over. I was still sitting on the edge of Luke's desk, feeling exposed and stunned, and Luke was sagging against the desk next to me, all the life gone out of him.

"My God," he murmured, massaging his brow as though trying to get rid of a headache. He had put his shirt back on so quickly that the buttons were wrongly matched, and his collar hung on him at a cockeyed angle. "Emily, I'm so, so sorry..."

"It's alright," I said hoarsely. "It's like I told Olivia—"

"It's not alright," he said firmly and looked over to me. I couldn't read his expression, and that terrified me. Was he angry at me? At himself? "I should never have put my hands on you. I took advantage of you and I—"

"Luke, please, you didn't take advantage of anyone. I wanted that just as much as you did. I haven't been able to stop thinking about you since I started working here."

Luke passed his hands over his face and groaned heavily. He looked almost like he was in pain.

"Emily, you can't just say things like that. I'm your boss. And for God's sake, you're nineteen years old."

"I'm grown," I shot back. "And I'm legal. You didn't seem to have a problem with my age a few minutes ago."

"What happened a few minutes ago should never have happened, and now Olivia is involved. I don't want this to keep spiraling out of control, and apparently, neither of us can hold back when we're around each other. I'm sorry, Emily. You're a wonderful girl, and obviously, I am very attracted to you. But I don't think it's a good idea for us to be alone together anymore."

His words were like a smack in the face. Hot tears burned in my eyes, threatening to fall.

"What about the photos? The project?"

"We're still going to use your work, and you're still going to be properly credited for it. And I'll look for future photography opportunities for you at the company that don't involve me, I promise. But you acting as my photographer is just too intimate. I'm sorry."

I felt numb all over as I pushed myself off his desk and

stood unsteadily. All the thrill and arousal from before had soured in my stomach and turned to shame and anger. I snatched my panties up off the floor and stuffed them into my purse, yanking up my camera bag as I smoothed down my dress. I tried to do all this without facing Luke so he wouldn't see me cry.

"Emily," he began, so softly that it felt like pins and needles being stuck into my heart.

"It's fine," I croaked. "You're right. I was stupid."

"I never said that."

"Olivia did. And she's right. I know better than this. I think it would be best if you didn't talk to me, please, or call. Just... not for a little while."

Luke's face crumpled, and he straightened as though he was about to come to me and take me in his arms. But he didn't move.

"I respect that. I will respect your wishes, Emily. And none of this will threaten your position here. This will not get out; I swear it."

"Thank you," I managed, gathering up the last of my things from the office. An hour ago, I had been on top of the world, sitting in a circle of top-level executives who were praising my work while Luke's hand was on my knee. He had smiled at me so genuinely when I suggested solutions to the Dallas problem, with a warmth I would never have expected from a man with a reputation for being unemotional and calculating. Now the memory was ruined, and everything felt terrible. All I wanted to do was run home and curl up in my bed and cry. But I knew that wasn't possible. I still had a job to do, and now I had to avoid raising suspicion. I could only pray that no one had heard our tryst, but heads would definitely turn if I rushed out of Luke's office crying after a lengthy private meeting and then left the office for the day.

Luke drifted over to me as I made my way to the door, hand hovering protectively over the small of my back. But he didn't dare touch me, not after what we had done and what Olivia had seen.

"Take care of yourself," he said, weakly I thought. Then he opened the door for me, and I walked out into the office with my shoulders back, and my head held high. I had wiped the tears from my face and didn't make eye contact with anyone as I clipped over to my desk and took my seat. I also didn't glance back at Luke.

My head was swimming, and I knew that there was no way I was going to get any work done for the rest of the day. I hadn't been brave enough to look at Olivia when I passed by, but when I looked up, I saw she was doing her best to avoid watching me, even though I kept catching nervous glances from the corner of her eye. Had she really been upset enough to report Luke for indecency with an employee? I didn't know her well enough to be sure, but Luke seemed to, and I found myself increasingly grateful for the non-disclosure agreement he made her sign. I resolved to go to the bathroom, splash some water on my face, and put my underwear back on to make sure that I at least felt decent enough for the rest of my day. As I stood to go, I saw from the clock hung on the wall that it was only 10:30. I sighed heavily — what a way to start the workday.

Chapter Eleven

LUKE

The next week was slow torture. True to my word, I gave Emily a wide berth. I avoided her desk, didn't meet her eyes for more than a polite second in the halls and waited for another lift if I saw she was in an elevator. It was impossible not to see the hurt in her eyes as she dropped her gaze when I passed by, giving me only the smallest smile so as not to hint at any impropriety. It twisted my gut to see her removing herself from my path, but what was I supposed to do about it? We had committed the ultimate indiscretion together. If anyone other than Olivia walked into that room and found us together, it would have destroyed her career. I had to be more careful. If I really gave a damn about her, I should always keep it in the forefront of my mind that I was her employer and she was my employee. I held all the power in this relationship and any fallout from what happened between us would come down squarely on her head. It wasn't fair. But I knew by now that very little about life was.

Still, I couldn't get her out of my head. If I thought that finally consummating our desire for each other would be enough to burn the thought of her out of my mind, I was dead wrong. The intrusive thoughts of her smile or her face rapt with pleasure increased, as did my shameful nighttime fantasies of her hips and mouth and lovely searching hands. I felt like a damn high school student. Even the mention of her name was enough to send me tail-spinning into forbidden thoughts. And more than that, I worried about her. I wondered how she was processing what happened between us, or if Olivia treated her any differently now, and even if she could move past what happened to her the night her car had been stolen. I was in too deep, obsessed, and preoccupied, and I needed to do something about it. But what could I do?

The opportunity came a week later after Olivia came into my office on Monday to do our usual weekly run-down. She was still being chilly with me, but tiredly, showing more of her exhaustion with work than any real anger at me. Catching me with one of my interns was just another extra strain that wasn't in her job description, one of the dozen things she was being asked to shoulder as our new product launch and the opening of our Dallas location consumed the entire SkyBlue office. I felt terrible for her and resolved to insist she take a vacation as soon as I could spare her.

We didn't talk much beyond business that day, but she did remind me that I had agreed to a speaking engagement in San Francisco.

"California?" I demanded, as though angry that the state would even dare to exist.

"You said you would go, and I confirmed your attendance last week. Sorry."

"Olivia, I'm swamped, I can't—"

"We're all drowning, Luke. Listen, I've done my best to keep the press conferences and speaking invitations at bay, but eventually, you're going to have to go to one of them. The conference in San Francisco is perfect. You can kill a lot of birds with one stone and be back in forty-eight hours. I know you can do this."

I sighed, massaging my brow. Olivia was seated in one of the nearby chairs, legs crossed primly as she sipped a triple Americano. Her coffee consumption probably funded all the cafes within a mile radius. Her lipstick this week was a deep berry, and it stained her cup like a smear of blood, which was appropriate since she seemed ready to rip anyone's throat out without a moment's notice. In all honesty, I was too.

"Do I have to tell them you've come down with something horrible," she asked with a sigh.

"No, no," I said, waving away the out she had given me. "I'll go, you're right. As usual."

"Good. I'll get the itinerary in order, and I'll be there at the airport to meet you the morning of the flight, as usual. You're going to be fine, Luke. Just shake hands and give your speech and pose for as many photographs as they want, and then you can come home."

Photographs. The word stirred in my mind, hatching a plot that I knew I would enact even before I thought whether or not it was a good idea.

"Olivia..." I began. She glanced up from her papers, dark eyes searching.

"What is it?"

"I don't want you to come along on this one."

An ashen pallor came over her dark skin. "What?"

"It's not that you aren't a huge help to me!" I said quickly.

"You're the best there is, honestly, but you're burning yourself out. You're frayed down to the wire, Liv."

"I'm not—"

"Yes, you are. I've been pushing you to the brink the last few months and I know I'm a hypocrite, but you need to take a step back. I'm afraid if I take you to San Francisco you'll drop dead on me or something. You're excellent at your job, but it isn't essential for me to take my assistant along to every conference. I'll manage, really."

"Really?" She said, one skeptical brow creeping towards her hairline. She had never been good at letting other people take over her duties. Arguably, she was worse at it than I was. "You'll be fine with no one to pull your schedule together or call the hotels or arrange dinner reservations or—"

"I'll take Sonia instead. She's a social butterfly; she loves these sorts of things. She can handle an itinerary just fine."

"And what am I supposed to do here while you and Sonia try not to burn down San Francisco?"

I couldn't help but smile at this. Olivia's dry wit always brightened my mood, no matter the circumstances.

"Rest. You might have to look up the meaning of the word in the dictionary, but I think you can figure it out. Take some half days. Hell, take the whole day off. We're past the launch now; the public reaction is out of our hands. You've done everything you could and then some. I want you to rest. I want you well."

Olivia wanted to stick up for herself, to insist that she was happy to work until she dropped, but I saw her eyes soften. She needed this, and she knew it.

"What's going on with you, huh? Usually, you're Mr. Asshole, and now suddenly, you're the soul of charity."

"I wouldn't go that far. You're more useful to me alive than dead, so really I'm being selfish."

"That sounds more like it," she said, sweeping to her feet. "Alright. I'll take a step back on this one. I'll email Sonia and make sure she's available. I'll brief her to high heaven before the two of you leave and transfer over all your scheduling details to her phone."

"You're a Godsend."

"Yes I am," she said over her shoulder, and then disappeared back to her desk.

I waited a full minute before I retrieved my phone and pulled up my contacts, my mouth dry. I scrolled until I found Emily's name and then typed out a simple message.

Are you free this weekend?

Chapter Twelve

EMILY

*I*f I was honest with myself, I hadn't expected to hear from Luke again. It didn't matter how tenderly he spoke to me the last time I saw him, or how passionate he had been when he took me, or even that we worked in the same building and had to pass each other in the halls awkwardly. He made the fact that we could not be trusted together quite clear. As angry as I was with him for saying it out loud, I knew he was right. No amount of good sense could keep me from looking at Luke Thorpe in a way that wasn't appropriate for the workplace or fantasizing about his hands on my body, and probably not from offering myself to him the moment he asked. It was safer for us to be apart, and I appreciated him respecting my request for space. I knew that eventually, we would have to talk again and move past things, but the two weeks of silence helped me to breathe again. Not that I particularly wanted to, but Olivia had been right. I was smart enough to know that Luke was trouble, and we both needed space to think.

When his name lit up my phone on Monday morning, I could hardly believe it. Heart pounding, I read his message. This weekend? Was he asking me out on a date? A second later, another message followed.

I have a speaking engagement in San Francisco and need a photographer. I wondered if you would be interested.

Interested was putting it lightly. I was well beyond interested in advancing my career, and in seeing Luke again, but the last time those two things happened, the results had been explosive. I hadn't been able to stop thinking about the way he felt inside me, the way his hands burned fingerprints into my skin. There was no forgetting it. I couldn't go a single day without losing myself to the memory. I couldn't sleep; I would always end up writhing in the dark under the oppressive weight of the memory, aching for release. My stomach dropped every day as I rode the elevator up to work. Would I see him today? Would he ever speak to me again?

I guess his text answered that question.

I stared at the screen for another minute. Surely he wasn't inviting me along on a private trip? That would go against what he said the last time we spoke.

I leaned out over my desk to peek around the edge of my cubicle. The door to Luke's office was closed, as usual. Olivia was typing away at her desk as though nothing had happened. Did she know he had asked me to travel with him? Something told me he probably hadn't wanted to have that conversation since it would have surely turned into a screaming match.

I glanced back down at the phone in my hand, suddenly nervous that anyone might pass by and read the text over my shoulder.

I might be, I typed back. *How long would we be gone?*

Just one night. Sonia is coming along as well.

I breathed out a little sigh of relief, then realized with a twinge of guilt that I was disappointed as well. The last thing I needed in my life right now was unchaperoned time with Luke, but that didn't mean that it didn't sound appealing to some foolishly animal part of my brain.

I don't have any other plans. I'd be happy to come along and snap some photos.

Great. We're meeting at the airport at five am on Saturday morning. I can send a car around to pick you up from your apartment if you'd like.

The offer seemed insanely lavish for someone in my paygrade, but it must seem like nothing to Luke, who lived in a world of private cars and valet parking and penthouse suites. I couldn't imagine what the accommodations would be like if we were traveling on the company dime. Like the handbags Olivia and Sonia sported, it seemed needlessly luxurious, but I had to admit that it also sounded appealing.

Maybe hanging out with the girls in the office was rubbing off on me.

That would be perfect.

Send your address over to Sonia, and she'll handle the scheduling. Looking forward to having you as part of the team on this trip.

His texts were so succinct and business like, the complete opposite of the sweet words he used on me in his office a few weeks ago. I desperately wanted to go to him, to knock on his door and ask what precisely this offer meant for us, but I knew that if he decided to text instead of call or walk out and talk to me himself, he wanted some distance. He was doing his best not to treat me indecently, and I should respect that. Saturday would come soon enough. And then, under Sonia's watchful eye, I would figure out what this offer was about.

The crack of dawn on Saturday came earlier than anyone wanted it to, but I was up, dressed, and standing out on my front stoop with my bags in hand five minutes before the car arrived for me. I had my camera charged and ready to go in the satchel slung across my body, and I cradled it in my lap like a baby as I rode to the airport in tinted-window, leather-interior comfort. The car, shiny black with a partition between the front and back seats, was nicer than any I had ever ridden in, and it certainly beat the subway. I expected to be dropped off at one of the major airline terminals as we drew into the early morning traffic of La Guardia, but instead, my driver pulled around to a part of the airport I had never been to before. He got out before me and opened my door to help me out, popping the trunk and rolling my suitcase down a narrow strip of concrete. We were, to my surprise, not heading to a gate at all. We were walking straight toward a private jet.

I swallowed hard. There was no way this was happening. I knew that Luke was rich but seriously? A private jet?

Sonia was already there, looking breezy and runway ready in a cherry colored jumpsuit and tall strappy heels. A white snake-skin purse emblazoned with the Marc Jacobs logo shone on her hip. She gave me a jaunty wave from her position near the stair-case that led up to the jet's interior.

"Just in time! We'll be departing in about a half hour. Come on in; I'll show you around."

I tried not to let my wonder show as I allowed one of the flight attendants to take my bags and followed Sonia up the stairs to the lap of luxury that I would sit in for the better part of the morning.

"Luke's already inside," Sonia said over her shoulder. "He'll be happy to see you. He's so glad he doesn't have to put up with a bunch of press photos from people he doesn't know. He can be very private about things."

"Sure," I said weakly. It was hard not to think about what Luke and I had done in private. He opened himself up to passion when the eyes of the world were off him.

The jet's interior was as lavish as any rap song would have led me to believe it would be, albeit lacking in gaudy additions. Lushly carpeted floors sat beneath plush leather chairs that swiveled to face each other, and someone had set a tray with orange juice and scones out on one of the glass-topped tables. Subtle, naturalistic lighting and discreet matte black speakers set into the walls made the room feel more like the lobby of an upscale hotel than the passenger area of a plane. And in the middle of it all, sitting, feet up on an ottoman with a newspaper fanned out in front of him, was Luke.

He glanced up at us, and for a moment, our eyes met, green on blue. He held my gaze for a fraction of a second longer than was necessary and then said, with a courtesy that could only be described as professional, "Emily. Good to see you. How was the drive over?"

Sonia deposited herself carelessly in the seat across from Luke, leaving the one in the aisle next to him open for me. I hesitated next to it for a moment before I lowered myself down.

"Just fine, thanks. Wonderful, actually. Your driver is very thoughtful."

"He's one of the best. I'm glad he treated you right. I hope you got some sleep before the flight."

I tucked my camera bag under my seat. I wasn't sure if the same in-flight protocol applied to private jets as it did to commercial airlines, but I wanted to make sure I didn't make a faux pas.

"A little. I kept waking up, though."

Thinking about you, I wanted to add. And your mouth and your hands and your —

"Good luck sleeping on the flight," Sonia put in. "It doesn't matter how cushy these private planes are; I can never get any shut-eye suspended thousands of feet in the air."

"Do you have flight anxiety?" I turned to Sonia when I asked her this, hoping that taking my eyes off Luke would take my mind off him as well.

"Not with two shots of tequila in me," she said with a wicked smirk and waved over a flight attendant who had been waiting in the wings.

The flight was beyond comfortable. I had never enjoyed such elegant accommodations in my entire life, and I tried not to gawk at the giant flat screen television that appeared from the ceiling mid-flight, or the baskets of hot almond croissants, bagels, and muffins that were wheeled out after we reached altitude. They offered me champagne, which I declined for fear of looking like a lush, but Luke ordered himself a mimosa and insisted I have whatever I liked, especially since it was a long flight to San Francisco. So I followed his lead and sipped champagne and orange juice and nibbled on a croissant while trying to ignore how much he was staring at me — studying, really, with a look of amused delight tugging at the corners of his mouth.

"Have you ever been on a private jet before?" He asked me once the attendants had retreated to the back of the plane. His voice was gentle, sitting in that warm place that I heard when he was congratulating me and yanking down the zipper on my dress. If it had been anyone else, I would think they were making fun of me, but Luke just seemed curious.

"No," I admitted. "Am I staring an awful lot?"

"Just a little," he said with a chuckle. "But it's okay. It's alright to enjoy things. I remember the first time I got onto one of these. I never wanted to leave again."

I glanced over to Sonia. She was definitely still awake but was dozing with her chin in her hand, and a silky eye mask pulled down over her face.

"It is pretty amazing. Do you fly everywhere like this?"

"No, only when I need to get somewhere quickly and need privacy, or when I'm doing a long haul international trip and don't want to spend fourteen hours cramped between two other sleep-deprived businessmen on a commercial flight."

"Sounds fair to me," I said, taking another sip of my drink. Luke's green eyes roamed over my face, and I felt my cheeks growing hot. Why couldn't I control my blushing around him for ten minutes? It was a dead giveaway of my emotions and always had been. But Luke didn't seem bothered. He just cut into his English muffin and egg and smiled over at me.

"I'm happy you could make it. On short notice, of course."

"Of course! I was happy to get your text. About the job, I mean," I added quickly.

Luke's smile didn't fall away, but his face was inscrutable. What was he thinking? Had he been thinking about me the same way I thought about him? Or had he put our illicit encounter out of his mind entirely, just added it to a list of lousy past decisions? Had he found someone else to warm his bed and take his mind off his intern? I didn't have much to offer a man in his position, after all, and I had almost jeopardized his career.

"Good," he said and turned back to his newspaper. We chatted again on and off during the flight, but mostly Luke went over his speech with Sonia, highlighting weak spots and making last-minute adjustments. I listened to him practice stirring words about innovation and change, and I couldn't help but feel a pang of swelling pride in my chest. He truly was an exceptional man and one who believed in people and their dreams so much. I had no idea how I was supposed to get over him when he was so close to me, speaking so eloquently about the things he cared about. So I listened, miserable, and delighted at the same time.

It was dreary and overcast in San Francisco when we arrived, which put Sonia off her mood a bit. She grumbled about Luke's promise of California sunshine as our bags were being unloaded onto the tarmac, but he didn't seem sympathetic.

"I told you it wasn't a vacation," he said simply.

"Yeah," Sonia countered. "And Olivia made it sound like she was sending me into the front lines of a world war, so who was I supposed to believe?"

"Just get me to where I need to go, and I promise there'll be plenty of time for sightseeing later."

The three of us waited at the front of the airport for our rental cars, Sonia and I loitered protectively over the bags while Luke lost himself in answering work emails. When a shiny black car that looked exactly like the one that picked me up from my apartment pulled up alongside the curb in front of us, Sonia rolled Luke's bag towards the trunk. But then he looked up and shook his head.

"Sonia, I want you to take this one and go on a few errands before you head to the hotel. There's a short list of things I need picked up on your phone; Olivia should have sent it over. And call the venue; make sure they set everything for the conference."

"Are you sure?" Sonia asked, reluctantly taking the keys from the rental attendant who had driven the car over from the garage. "Olivia said not to let you out of my sights..."

"Olivia worries too much. I'll be fine, I promise. I've got Emily. We'll go straight to the hotel and get checked in, and I'll get a little work in before we all meet up for lunch. The errands shouldn't take too long."

"Alright," she said warily, her dark eyes skimming over me before she got into the car. I stiffened instinctively. Did she suspect something?

But if Sonia wondered about Luke's reason for wanting to be alone with me, she kept her thoughts to herself. Within minutes she disappeared into the car and pulled out into the steady stream of midday traffic, leaving me alone with my bag and the last man on Earth I could be trusted with.

I considered saying something, looking over at him and even opening my mouth to ask why he would send Sonia off by herself. But I never got the chance to ask, as a black car identical to the one Luke called for Sonia pulled up alongside us. Luke was still engrossed in whatever email he was reading and hardly glanced up as he handed his bag off to the valet who placed it alongside mine in the trunk.

"Emily, will you drive?" Luke asked lightly, already moving to sit in the passenger side of the car before I had time to answer. The valet deposited the keys in my sweating hands, hardly looking at my face. He probably did this fifty times a day and didn't bother to register the expressions of the people he passed cars onto. I couldn't blame him. But as he left me there standing stock-still on the sidewalk with keys weighing down my hands and Luke waiting for me in the car, I felt very alone.

How could I explain to Luke that I couldn't drive this car? I really couldn't? If I got behind the wheel, I might start shaking, or crying, or flinching from the images that flashed across my mind's eye no matter where I was or what job I had to do. I would have to explain my entire carjacking, and there was no guarantee that he would understand, even if I went through all the trouble and anxiety. My mother still insisted that I was experiencing the aftereffects of trauma, that I should see a therapist, and even though I knew she was right, talking about the incident with anyone seemed too intimidating to handle. Now, it looked like I would have to.

Taking a deep breath, I stepped off the curb and walked around to the driver's side of the car. Without saying a word to Luke, I slid into the seat and slotted my keys into the ignition. The first thin tendrils of panic rose up in my throat, making my breathing shallow, but I did my best to push them back down. This was so simple. I knew how to do this. All I had to do was turn the key and—

I started involuntarily as the engine rumbled to life. I knew that this car was better made than any I had ever been in and had an engine that purred like a kitten, but the sound grated on my ears like the roar of a monster. My face grew hot as the walls of the car pressed in tighter and tighter, and I had to force the memory of someone wrenching open my car door and throwing me out onto the street from my mind. Luke was still tapping away at his phone, oblivious to my distress. I took a deep breath, trying to force air into my screaming lungs, and put the car into gear.

I had to squeeze my fingers around the knob of the gearshift to keep them from shaking, but they were trembling freely as I brought them up to grip the steering wheel. I swallowed hard into my dry throat, eyes darting out onto the road. I felt sure that if I moved this car one inch panic would rise up to swallow me whole, but I had to drive, I had to get us to the hotel without breaking down, I had to—

"Emily?"

Luke had looked up from his phone, how long ago I wasn't sure and was looking at me with concern in his deep green eyes. His expression was strangely grave, although I expected him to be annoyed. He blacked out the screen on his phone with a click and slid it away into his briefcase.

"Are you alright?"

I turned to him, doing my best to keep a stiff upper lip, but when I spoke, my voice came out in a croak.

"I'm fine."

God, the tears were coming now, white-hot and irrepressible. I scrubbed the back of my hand against my eyes in an attempt to hold them back, but it was too late. The lump in my throat had grown painfully large, and I knew that it was only a matter of seconds before I was sobbing outright. In front of Luke Thorpe. In a car that probably cost more than the sum of my student loans. Oh God, why did this have to happen now?

"No, you're not," he said, using the same decisive voice he had when praising me, or telling me he wanted me or telling me that we couldn't be alone together again. "Get out of the car, Emily."

"I'm so sorry," I said, crying freely now as I unbuckled my seat belt. I was relieved I wouldn't have to drive but devastated that I hadn't been able to keep it together for him. I felt like I had made nothing but mistakes in our short time together and was proving myself to be a company liability again and again.

"Why are you sorry? There's nothing to be sorry about; I shouldn't have asked you to drive. Here, swap with me. I'll drive to the hotel."

"I can do my best to drive. I didn't mean to get so scared, I just—"

"It's really alright. Please, let me drive. I hate to see you like this."

With that, he was out of the car and around to my side, pulling open my door. I shuddered and cried out even though I didn't want to, pressed my eyes tight against the intrusive memories. Luke helped me out of the car with as much gentleness as he could manage and even swept one arm over my shoulders in a quick embrace before we went our separate ways. His fingers smoothed my hair down the back of my head, his green eyes tender as I cried like a fool, and in one electric moment, I realized a possibility that had only been a dim dream in my unconsciousness before now.

His protective, tall form was standing close to me on the street while I cried, and those piercing green eyes... Luke said he shouldn't have asked me to drive... Did that mean he knew about the carjacking and my PTSD? Was it possible that Luke was the man in black on the motorcycle that night who picked me up off the street and drove me safely home?

I felt a little unbalanced as I walked over to my side of the car, heart still pounding with anxiety, head swimming with realizations, but in the blink of an eye the door was shut behind me, and we were pulling out into San Francisco traffic with Luke at the wheel. He kept glancing over to me every few seconds to make sure I was alright, and I dabbed at my eyes while I leaned my head back against the headrest. I had only been in California for twenty minutes, and I was already exhausted. I wanted to go home. But most of all, I wanted to know the truth.

"I'm sorry," I said again. Even though I knew that he would insist again that it wasn't my fault, I didn't know what else to say.

"I get overwhelmed sometimes. When I get behind the wheel of a car."

"I can see that," he murmured, changing lanes and taking the exit that would lead us to our hotel. "Did you... Is it alright if I ask if something happened to you in a car? A bad experience or an accident?"

He was trying to appear as though he had no idea what could have caused my distress, but he had already shown his hand when he knew to take over driving. Luke being the man who saved me might be a crazy long shot, but everything he said in the last few minutes cemented my suspicions.

"I was carjacked," I said at last, letting out a shaky breath. "But I think, if I'm not wrong, that you might already know that."

Luke didn't look over to me or indicate that he had been found out, or that he was surprised by my accusation. Instead, he said,

"I'm sorry I didn't mention anything earlier. You didn't seem to remember me, and I didn't want you to feel cornered."

The weight of realization settled over me. Luke had been there that night, he had seen me torn from my car and thrown to the ground, and he had been the one who pulled me up with his strong leather-clad hands. He was the subject of my girlish daydreams, the scorching nighttime fantasies that got me panting and writhing underneath my sheets as I urged myself on to climax. I felt stunned and half awake. This wasn't possible; it couldn't be. And yet here I was, sitting in a car with a man who seemed to understand my terrors and my needs instinctively. A man who I let take me in his arms and fuck me on the edge of his desk just two weeks ago.

"God," I breathed, bringing a hand to my forehead. It felt hot.

Luke's nervous eyes jumped over to me.

"I should have told you sooner, and I'm sorry about that. Are you feeling alright? You don't look so hot."

"No, no, I'm fine..." I had thrown the words out casually but was surprised to find that they were true. Despite my shock, and the jittery fear still coursing through my veins from my near-panic attack minutes ago, I felt better. More settled, as though all the disparate, jagged pieces of my life were starting to come together. "It feels good to know, finally."

"Did you just figure it out?"

"Yeah... I guess that makes me pretty stupid."

"No, not at all. I didn't realize who you were until we were together in the elevator for the first time, you probably don't remember—"

"I remember," I said with a laugh. I certainly remembered making a fool of myself in front of him. He stared at me with such an intensity I could practically feel his eyes moving over my body. I spent the whole day beating myself up for making such a bad impression on the CEO, not realizing that he was probably spending our short ride together deliberating whether to identify himself as the man on the motorcycle.

"God, this is all so... It's just...."

"A bit much, I know," Luke said soothingly. His voice wasn't authoritative at all. Instead, it was so soothing and gentle that I wanted to cry again. Was this how he would talk to me if I weren't his employee, if I had invited him up to my room that night after the carjacking, or if we had met in a cafe like two ordinary people and started a conversation? I would never know, because now he was my boss, and he was driving me to an industry conference where I would be expected to keep things professional and photograph him for hours on end.

"Yeah," I said, sagging against the car door. "I feel like I got the wind knocked out of me. It's not bad, though. I'm glad to know, and I guess I am happy it was you all along. But I'm... tired."

"The hotel is just up ahead; you're free to go up to your room, splash some water on your face, and rest before we head out again."

"Actually could you just pull over, maybe? I want a few minutes to pull myself together again before I see Sonia. Is that alright?"

"Of course," Luke said, and swerved off towards the nearest exit. Within moments he found a quiet parking lot for us to loiter in, well away from the hustle and bustle of the busy city, and he leaned back in his seat with a sigh as he put the car in park. When he looked over at me, eyes shining, I could see he was tired too. But he also looked at me like I was the most delicate thing in the world, like I was something valuable to him, and that also made me want to cry.

Chapter Thirteen

LUKE

The parking lot of a value grocery store wasn't exactly an ideal place for a heart-to-heart, but that's where Emily and I found ourselves, taking deep breaths in the hot, quiet interior of a car. Her face was still red from crying, but now her eyes were shining with some other emotion that I couldn't place: wonder, maybe, or fear. I was surprised to find that I was actually nervous, as nervous as I might have been taking my first date to prom. I had no idea whether Emily was upset with me for keeping this from her or not. I debated telling her countless times, but every time I convinced myself that there was no way to do it that didn't come across as invasive and inappropriate. Then again, I suppose I had been plenty invasive and inappropriate with her in the short time that we knew each other, as Olivia could testify.

Now I reached across the armrest and took her small hand in mine. It was clammy from fear, but she warmed under my touch as I rubbed small circles into her skin with my thumb.

"I should have told you sooner," I said quietly. "You deserved to know."

Emily fixed me with those huge blue eyes, and the sight took my breath away. Then she leaned over and kissed me sweetly on the mouth.

Her lips were warm and flushed from crying, so gentle and exploratory on mine. This was nothing like the passionate kisses we shared in my office. This was a tender, almost chaste, a kiss of forgiveness, and I didn't bring my hands up to touch her face for fear of ruining how perfect it was. I should have known this would happen from the moment we got into the car together, but I was still taken aback. Somehow, in all my dreams of Emily, I had never imagined her like this, so giving and so open and so absolutely vulnerable with me.

"Emily," I said softly, with her breath still in my mouth and her nose nudging against mine.

"I'm not mad at you," she said. "You were just doing what you felt was right. And honestly, I don't know what I would have done if I had known before now."

"I didn't want you to feel like I was stalking your or that I had singled you out. I tried to give you your space."

"I appreciate that," she said, drawing back into her corner of the car. She had a light dusting of pink across the tops of her cheeks now like her boldness scandalized her. I loved her like this, earnest and honest about what she was feeling.

"What were you even doing out there in Queens in the middle of the night?" She asked. "That run-down neighborhood is the last place I'd expect to see a guy like you zipping around on his fancy motorbike."

I leaned against my side of the car as well and glanced over to her. She wanted her space now, but she also wanted to know more about my story. This, I felt, was the next step necessary in our intimacy, whatever shape that was taking. I was willing to give it to her, and anything else she wanted or needed from me. Sonia would be arriving at the hotel soon, looking for both of us, but I didn't care. She could check herself in and sleep off the early flight for a little while.

"I actually grew up there. I was having dinner with a couple of old friends who still live in the area."

Emily's eyebrows shot up. "You're from my neighborhood?"

"Not exactly. But I'm from the area. Born and raised for the first eighteen years of my life. I didn't leave until I moved into my college dorm."

"That's... not exactly what I expected from you."

I smiled wryly, leaning my head against the knuckles of one hand.

"Most people don't unless they've known my family for some time. They see the car and the press photos, and they assume I've been wealthy my whole life. But nothing could be further from the truth."

So I told her. I told her everything there was to know about my childhood, about my mother's death and my father's drinking, and the kindness of Aunt Martha. I told her about Nico and Marcus and everyone else in the neighborhood, their big Friday night meals, and raucous jokes and the games we would play in the street together. Emily told me she had grown up in the New Jersey suburbs, and she seemed enchanted about my stories of summers in the city getting in trouble for opening fire hydrants or throwing water balloons at passing cars.

"I wish I had been brave enough to do that when I was a kid," Emily said with a wicked smirk. "All I ever did was study and draw and text my friends."

"It isn't the same anymore," I conceded. "Kids now don't get outside and play like they used to; they aren't allowed. It isn't as safe; I don't think. God, listen to me. I'm making myself sound ancient. 'The kids these days.' Kill me now."

Emily giggled, the peal of silver bells.

"Just a little. But I don't mind. I like hearing about how things are different and the same."

"I promise you; I'm not *that* old."

"Oh, I know," she said breezily, and then paled a little when she realized what she had given away. I smirked at her.

"How do you know how old I am? Been doing a little after-hours research on the boss?"

"I like to know all I can about the company I'm working for," she said, bristling, but there was a smile threatening to break through her self-possessed veneer.

"And about its CEO, apparently."

"Well.... maybe. But I don't think 32 is very old. Not to me, anyway."

Her voice was soft, nervous, and I knew what she was trying to say. That she didn't think I was too old for her. She thought we could continue with whatever was going on between us without worrying about the age difference. I wanted to gently correct her, tell her that she could do much better for herself with someone in her own age group and season of life, but her gentle invitation lit a fire in me that was hard to deny. I wanted to draw her close against me and kiss her slow and deep, to show her everything I had learned in over thirty years of life that I could use to please her. I wanted to feel her blossom like a flower under my hands while I learned the contours and particulars of her body, to watch her face color with that beautiful girlish flush.

But I kept my hands to myself.

"I appreciate that," I said.

Emily glanced down at her watch and made a distressed sound in the back of her throat.

"I'd guess we had better get back to the hotel, huh? Sonia probably thinks we're dead in a ditch somewhere."

I rolled my eyes as I put the rental car into gear. "Sonia probably had a double whiskey soda at the bar to soothe the last of her nerves from flying and is asleep in her bed, blissfully unaware that we never checked in; I'll bet you five dollars."

"Deal," Emily said with a laugh.

I grinned as I eased the car through the parking lot and back onto the highway, and I was taken aback, not for the first time, at how easily Emily brought a smile to my face. I was generally serious, and Olivia was always chiding me to smile more in meetings, so I didn't intimidate people so much, but it came easily when Emily was around. Everything she said delighted me, and all I could think about was how much I wanted to see her delighted.

"Luke?" She said a few minutes later.

"Yes?"

"Seriously though, the neighborhood where you grew up sounds nice. I've never lived in a place where everyone on the street knows each other like that and helps take care of each other. I know you said that it wasn't all roses, but I think it sounds beautiful."

Something inside my chest ached.

"Well, maybe, I'll take you there someday."

Emily smiled down at her hands and then looked out the window, and I could hardly believe the words coming out of my mouth. I was generally so guarded and so private, but the idea of showing Emily around the banged-up streets where I had grown up brought me genuine joy. What was this girl bringing out of me? And more importantly, was I going to be able to hide the way she affected me from the outside world for long?

"I'd like that," she said, and I felt like my heart was trying to crawl right out of my chest. This was definitely not optimal. I had been kissing my college intern in a rental car on a company trip, and now I was making promises to introduce her to my home turf. Worst of all, I wanted to keep those promises. I wanted to watch her smile and ask questions as we walked around my old neighborhood, and I wanted her to meet Aunt Martha, who was always calling to check in and nag me about not having settled down with anyone yet. This was very not good.

"Your family must be very proud of you," Emily said. Guilt nibbled at the back of my brain, but I tried to put it out of my mind.

"Oh, they are. They wish they saw me more, but they are."

"A bit of a workaholic?"

"I think you already know the answer to that question."

"I don't think I've ever gotten into the office before you," she mused. "And you're always there when I leave at night. I know it must take a lot of hours to keep SkyBlue up and running at capacity, but I'm sure it gets draining sometimes."

"Sometimes," I admitted and realized just how tired I was. The last few weeks weighed on my shoulders like a barbell, threatening to pull me down into total burnout. But burnout was never an option. I had to keep it together for my company and my employees.

"That woman I saw with the little boy in your office the day I brought you your coffee, was that the sister you mentioned?"

"Yes, Sarah. The little boy is her son, Ryan."

"She seemed pretty upset. Is everything alright between the two of you?"

The corners of my mouth tightened.

"It's fine. We sometimes squabble but... it's fine. I lose track of why we argue as soon as the argument is over. I don't have a lot of time for trivial things."

Emily glanced over at me sidelong, and even while driving, I could tell she had a thoughtful gleam in her eye.

"Does that mean I'm not meaningless to you? You've gone out of your way to spend an awful lot of time on me in the last month or so."

I swallowed hard. I wasn't going to be able to keep up the charade of not letting on how preoccupied I had been with her for long.

No words came easily for me to say, but I reached out and took her hand instead. The warm weight of it felt right in my own.

Chapter Fourteen

EMILY

$\mathcal{P}$ulling up to an elite hotel with my hand in Luke Thorpe's was a surreal experience. He didn't pull away when we saw the valet. Instead, he took his time parking and then gave me a gentle squeeze before he disappeared out the driver's side door. I clung close to his side as we strolled into the gilded foyer of the hotel and checked into our rooms. The concierge smiled at both of us like we were a beautiful young couple on vacation. For one fleeting moment, I felt what it must be like to be Luke Thorpe's girlfriend, to be doted on and adored and envied by everyone who walked by. It was an intoxicating fantasy, one that felt like a powerful dream I never wanted to wake up from, and I struggled to remind myself that this wasn't real. Luke hadn't said anything about our kiss in the car, and for all I knew he might just be indulging me because he didn't want to hurt my feelings. He opened up to me about his past, sure, but there was no guarantee of affection in those words, no promise that we would see each other romantically or that we wouldn't see other people. I had to keep my head on straight. Otherwise, I would lose myself in how good this ocean of luxury and attention felt, and I might drown.

Luke's room was along the same hall as mine, a dozen or so doors down. He gave me a warm smile when he stopped by his own door but didn't reach out to touch me or invite me in. Instead, he just slotted his keycard into the door and wheeled his bags inside.

"Get some rest," he said. "You've had a trying day. The three of us will meet up later before the banquet, and then we can compare notes."

The three of us. I had almost convinced myself that Sonia wasn't here, that this was some sort of lover's retreat just for Luke and I. But I knew Sonia was nearby, sleeping off her flight anxiety in one of the luxurious rooms, and I knew that she would have questions when she woke up.

So I gave Luke my best upbeat smile and located my room, then threw myself down onto the fluffy white duvet as the door swung shut behind me.

What a morning. It wasn't even noon yet, and I felt like my heart had been through a steamroller. I needed to talk to someone. Someone who would listen without judging me, someone who was too far away to decide they needed to march over to my apartment as soon as I got home to tell me what bad choices I was making. I needed to process.

As usual, my little sister let the call ring through almost to voicemail before she picked up.

"Oh, hey, what's up?" She asked, as though I had just wandered into her bedroom and it startled her to see me there. It was something I had seen many times before, Darlene glancing up from her art tablet seated on the ground in that room with the walls plastered with magazine cutouts and band posters. It made me smile to imagine it.

"Oh, not a lot," I lied, hoping I sounded breezy. "You free right now?"

"Sure." I heard the distant wooden clattering of colored pencils being discarded. I must have caught her in the middle of one of her mammoth drawing projects. She probably had her hair pulled back in one of those ridiculous scrunchies she had rescued from the bottom of our mom's accessory box. She was very into the nineties now and thought mom jeans and technicolor windbreakers were all the rage.

"School going alright?"

"Alright as always. I got in trouble again last week for smoking out by my friend's car, even though we were technically off school grounds, so the charge was bogus. But my chemistry grade is back up, so that's good, I guess. It got mom off my case, anyway. How's work?"

"Oh... alright." I was fiddling with a long strand of my hair, winding it tightly around my finger before letting it spring loose. "Everything's good."

"Good."

Darlene wasn't stupid, and she knew I didn't just call to say hello. She was waiting me out, hoping to see what sort of gossip I had brought her.

"Actually..." I began warily. Was I really going to tell my little sister about this? But if not her, then who? "I'm actually in a bit of a weird situation at work right now."

"Oh yeah? What sort of situation?"

"Well, I've been sort of seeing this guy—"

"Oooooooh!"

"I said sort of, sort of! I don't know if it's serious or not yet, but we've had some... intense moments. And I see him fairly regularly. He's just so hard to read, and it's weird because, well... God, this will sound so crazy."

"I guarantee you it won't sound crazy," Darlene said with a snicker. "You should hear the stories my friends tell me. Seriously. I'm sorry for teasing. What's going on?"

"It's just that... this guy is my boss."

"Oh. Shit. Like your boss, boss? Like the guy directly over you? Because if he just works where you work, that's not so bad."

"No, he's definitely my boss. He's kind of... everyone's boss." I bit my lip and winced, bracing for impact. "He's actually the CEO."

"Holy shit!" Darlene crowed. "The CEO, are you serious? Like the big guy in charge for reals?"

"Keep your voice down!" I hissed. "Is mom there? I don't want her to—"

"Darlene?" I heard my mother's voice on the other end, muffled as though through a wall, and my heart dropped into my stomach. I had been so stupid to call home. I should have known better. I loved my mother, but she could never keep her nose in her own business, and as much as I liked talking to my sister, she was messy about secrets. "Is that your sister on the line with you?"

"It's nothing, Mom!" Darlene shouted back. "We're just chatting! Go away!"

"Ask her if she's thought more about that new car."

"No, I'm talking to Emily! You can talk to her later!"

"Alright, alright...."

There was the crackle of silence for a moment as Darlene waited for my mother's footsteps to disappear down the hallway. Then she returned to our call; voice pitched lower.

"Okay, sorry about that. CEO, Em? Are you kidding me?"

"No," I said miserably.

"How did it happen?"

"I don't know. Well, actually, I do, but it's a long and insane story. We met once outside of work before I got the job, but I didn't recognize him when I first started at SkyBlue. We just got thrown in together a couple of times, and one thing led to another and the next thing I knew—"

"Wait, a minute. SkyBlue?" I heard the insistent clicking of keys as Darlene looked up something on her laptop. Then she inhaled sharply. "Holy hell, I know this guy! He's that Elon Musk type dude with the smart cars. Isn't he like, ancient?"

"He's thirty-two," I shot back hotly. "Which is a very good age."

"Okay according to Wikipedia he's absolutely loaded. Look at you, turning into a sugar baby! Are you gonna get him to pay off your loans? You should get him to pay off your loans."

"Ugh, Darlene it's not like that. We're not an item and he's not my sugar daddy, we're just..."

"Boinking?"

"Ew, don't call it that! And no! Not currently and not in the future, I don't think. I don't know. There's just a lot going on and did you miss the part where I told you he was my boss? I'm hung up on my actual boss, Darlene, that's not good!"

I could practically hear her shrug on the other end.

"Maybe not, but you can't help the way you feel, can you? You can either ignore this guy and nurse your broken heart until it gets better or you can go after him, simple as that. Either can work, but you need to choose the one you can live with."

I pulled the fingernail out of my mouth that I had been gnawing on nervously.

"You give pretty good advice for a kid, did you know that?"

"I'm an old soul. Mom! What?"

By the sound of things, my mother had come back and was poking her head into Darlene's room.

"Will you let me talk to my daughter, please? You can't hog the phone all day."

"You have your own phone!"

"Two minutes, Darlene, and then I'll give it back! You've already got her on the phone."

"Uggggh, you're the worst! Here."

I started babbling protestations, not wanting to be passed off to my mother right now for love or money, but it was too late. I heard the awkward fumbling of a cell phone through hands, and then my mother's voice was on the other side, bright and uninvited.

"Hi, Bunny! How are you?"

"I'm fine Mom," I sighed. "Just trying to talk to Darlene."

"I know, I'll let you girls get back to it in a minute. Listen, have you thought any more about that new car? There's a Honda Civic one of our neighbors is selling cheap, if you want to come down and have a look at it."

I felt like tearing my hair out. I was appreciative for my mother's generosity, but now was not the time to discuss it, especially not after the incident in the rental car.

"A Civic sounds fine mom, really. I trust your judgment. Anything works for me. Can you give me back to Darlene, please?"

"It sounds like you've been seeing a guy," she said lightly, entirely ignoring my request. "He works in your same office, did I hear that right?"

"Mom. I told that to Darlene in confidence."

"I know, I know, I'll let you girls talk! You just know I have to put my two cents in, I'm just being a mom. But listen to me Emily, workplace romances are tricky. I don't know if this guy is in your department or what or if he's above or below you, but please, please be careful. This internship is too valuable to get thrown away for some guy."

"Of course I know that! I would never! That was actually what I was just telling Darlene if you would please give the phone back to my sister. I'm being smart about this Mom. I promise."

"Alright, alright. Just remember to think before you act. But you're a smart girl. You know I trust you. I love you, honey!"

"I love you too," I sighed. A moment later, I was returned to Darlene, who had probably gone red in the face with fury. I had been a very talkative and open daughter, often spending hours crying to my mother about crushes and friends. Darlene was much more private and preferred to express her emotions through art. She had a strict do-not-enter policy with my mother when it came to her bedroom.

"Mom's being the worst," she grumbled into the phone. "I'm gonna go before she eavesdrops more. But good luck out there! Don't do anything I wouldn't do."

"Sure, Darlene. Thanks for listening."

"Anytime. Later."

I sighed heavily as I tossed the phone aside, breathing out hard through my lips. I felt like I had been awake and wired for twenty-four hours, but it was barely afternoon. In a few hours, I knew I would have to go downstairs for professional networking and photo-snapping, looking my best and absolutely not looking at Luke for too long. I decided a shower would help me get there and treated myself to a long soak in the luxurious fountain shower provided by the hotel. Then I changed back into jeans and threw a thin T-shirt over my bare breasts, squeezing the water out of my hair with a towel.

It was at that moment I heard a crisp knock at my door.

I padded over to the door, my eyebrows drawn together in confusion. I hadn't ordered up room service, but I wasn't sure how these fancy hotels operated. For all I knew it was a bellboy come to bring hot towels or cucumber water or any of the other amenities that Luke's magical black card afforded us.

I opened the door. Luke Thorpe was leaning against my door frame, looking arrestingly attractive in slacks and shirt sleeves rolled up past his elbows. He had a dark, vulnerable look in his eyes that was at once hungry and pleading, and I could hardly breathe for how close he was to me, how unguarded he was being.

"I couldn't sleep," he said, never taking his eyes off my mouth. "Will you let me in, Emily?"

I knew what he was really asking me, what he was requesting permission to do. Every nerve in my body was on fire, singing a song of desire, and I shuddered in my thin, sheer t-shirt as his eyes fell from my mouth to my breasts to my bare feet. I was sure he had never looked better than he did now, looming over me with want written all over him, his jacket discarded, one of his beautiful long-fingered hands pressed against my door frame. There was no one else in the hallway. Sonia was nowhere to be seen. There was just us, just two people who no one knew worked together 3,000 miles away in New York.

"Yes," I whispered.

Luke's fingers slid through my hair and spread across the back of my head before I even closed the door behind him, pulling me in for a kiss I could drown in. I mumbled an incoherent protestation about the door, all I could manage with my head swimming from the taste of him, and he pushed the door shut behind us with one hand while circling my waist with the other.

He pulled me tightly against his body, so we were flush together, my painfully hard nipples brushed against his chest, my stomach pushing against his hardness. My body was already screaming out for him, my skin hypersensitive, my panties wet between my legs. I whimpered as he deepened our kiss, filling my mouth with his tongue, and I pulled him further into my room, towards my bed. I was going to have him, right here, right now. I was going to make that choice and deal with the consequences because this was too much of a good thing to pass up, and I didn't know if we would ever get a chance like this ever again.

"I couldn't stop thinking about you," Luke said, his lips chasing mine and trailing little kisses along my jaw. My head fell back, exposing my throat for his heated explorations.

"Tell me again," I pled, pulling his hands up, so they covered my breasts. Luke took his hands off me for one agonizing moment while he slipped them under my shirt, then he fondled me with enthusiasm as he kissed me.

"I can't stop thinking about you. I was sitting in that room, and all I could think of was how bad I wanted you, that's all I've been thinking about for weeks. I want to be inside you, Emily. I want to feel you writhe underneath me, and I want to make you come this time."

"Oh God," I groaned, clawing his shirt up over his head. His exposed chest offered itself to my searching mouth, and I kissed along every inch of exposed skin, committing the geography of his body to memory with my lips. I couldn't be close enough to him, couldn't kiss him thoroughly enough, even as I felt his breathing quicken in his chest. He groaned as I pressed my lips to his throat, the rumble of it traveling right through my body, and the next thing I knew I was being pushed back against the bed.

Luke tugged my shirt up over my head in one definitive yank, then leaned down to kiss me so softly. I thought I might cry as he laid me down on the thick hotel duvet. His broad palms spread over my stomach and my breasts, squeezing me gently as I whined and bucked my hips up towards him. I was soaking wet in my jeans and couldn't find any friction to help me towards the release I desperately needed. I felt like I could finish in seconds if I put my mind to it, I was so aroused, but I wanted to take this slow. I wanted to make it last, and I wanted to remember it.

I tugged Luke down over me and hooked my arms around his neck, slotting myself between his legs so I could grind against his hips slowly and intently.

"Fuck," he breathed into my mouth as I pressed our heat together, pressing up against his cock. He was already rock hard, and as huge as I remembered. I was desperate to feel him filling me up.

"Please," I begged as he slid his hands under my ass and pressed me up against him harder. I could feel him through my jeans now, rubbing against my most sensitive spot. I felt like a teenager rubbing out a quick, desperate orgasm with her boyfriend in the backseat of her parent's car, and the thought excited me even more. "Undress me. Please."

Luke didn't have to be told twice. He flicked my jeans open and pulled them off my legs with a few determined tugs, then slid his palm between my legs and circled my clit with a slow, firm pressure through my lace panties. I cried out so sharply the neighbors probably thought I was in pain, devolving into an incoherent, begging babble at the end.

"God! Luke, please please, I want you, just please—"

Luke hooked his thumbs under my panties and tugged them off, exposing me to his fingers.

"You're soaked," he purred, obviously pleased with himself, and then slid a finger inside me.

"Yes!" I exclaimed, digging my fingers into his back and pulling him in closer. "More, please—"

Another finger entered me, wide and rough, and I practically melted. He fucked me with his fingers deeply and slowly, kissing me languidly as I squirmed and panted. With every frenzied toss of my head, he chased me with his mouth, pulling me back into his intoxicating kiss as he sped up his rhythm. I had fingered myself to the memory of his touch before, but it paled in comparison to this.

"God, I'm not going to last if you go on like that. Please, I want you."

"Tell me what you want, Emily," he said into my neck. His voice was ragged with lust.

"I want you to fuck me like you did on your desk. Please."

That was all I could think to say, but this man could reduce me to begging with a single glance, no more than one kiss. His insistent pressure inside me disappeared, and I fell back against the pillows, struggling to catch my breath as residual pleasure coursed through me in waves. I was so close that I could finish myself off in seconds, but I breathed deeply and pulled myself together as Luke rid himself of the rest of the clothes. Then he was over me again, kissing me with insistence as he spread my legs, sank his fingers into the soft flesh of my hips, and sheathed himself inside me.

The sensation was immense, and I bucked my hips up against him, taking as much of his cock as I could. He fucked me deeply, pulling almost all the way out before pounding into me again. Together we set a steady, relentless pace, making a mess of ourselves and the sheets. I kissed and licked his sweat-slicked skin, desperate for more of him, and he fondled my breasts with the clumsy desperation of a man nearing his release.

"Just a little more," I pled. "I'm so close."

"You're gorgeous," He panted. "Let me see you come, sweetheart. Come for me."

He circled my clit with a finger still slick with my juices, but it was his words that put me over the edge. He spoke to me with such a gentle, irresistible command that any tension left in my body melted away instantly, opening me to the wave of orgasm that crashed over me.

"Oh God," I said, latticing our fingers together and squeezing. "I'm coming. I'm coming for you. Please don't stop."

"Fuck," he groaned. "I can feel you tightening around my cock. Fuck, Emily..."

I cried out his name in agonized pleasure when I finished, and he picked up his speed to an almost frantic pace. I relished the feeling of him fucking me past my orgasm, taking his own pleasure from my spent body, and a minute later, he groaned my name and spent himself inside me. I tightened my legs around him and pulled him down into a sticky, warm embrace, where we lay for the next minute, catching our breath together.

We kissed lazily for I don't know how long, nuzzling noses and breathing deeply together. I trailed my fingers down his back, feeling the firmness of his muscles, now relieved of all tension. His warm weight was like a security blanket, and I felt sure that I could sleep there beside him for a decade, tired and satisfied and perfectly safe.

Part of me couldn't believe what had happened. I had let Luke Thorpe into my hotel room. I let him touch me like that and take me on top of the covers when we were on a business trip with Sonia dozing in one of the rooms next door. But another part of me felt that this was inevitable. Luke and I had always been building up to this moment, blissed-out in each other's arms. Another tiny part of me was distressed because I just realized something important. I had realized, as I lay in his arms, twining my fingers lightly through his hair, that I might be doing the unthinkable without even meaning to.

I might be falling for Luke Thorpe.

Chapter Fifteen

LUKE

I did not understand how I had let this happen. It was impossible to say that I regretted it; this was the furthest feeling from regret I could fathom. Emily and I had wanted each other for months, and this was our opportunity to enjoy each other thoroughly. She had somehow broken through my carefully constructed defenses in the car. I saw no reason to deny ourselves any longer, especially not since she knew the truth of who I was to her. But a practical voice in the back of my head chided me for being so irresponsible, for jeopardizing both our careers. I hadn't thought this through all the way. Was I starting a relationship here? Initiating a one-off fling with an intern to blow off steam while traveling for a conference? I wasn't entirely sure what I wanted yet, but I knew it wasn't the latter. Emily was so much more to me than that, even if we still had a long way to go in getting to know each other. I didn't want to pull her into my orbit just to cast her off again, and I didn't want us to fall into a stifling rhythm of only talking to one another when we were lonely for adult company. That couldn't be the way this went, not if I had anything to say about it.

"That was amazing," Emily said finally. Her voice was so soft, like the sweet skin of a peach. "Thank you."

"What are you thanking me for?" I replied, amused. No one had ever thanked me after sex before, no matter what they thought of it.

Emily lifted her head, red hair falling in a tumble to one side. She kissed me, a feather-light pressure that was somehow even more intense than the passionate kiss we shared when she let me into her room. This was an undiluted vulnerability, and I felt like I could become drunk on it.

"For everything. For the ride home, and the job, and the meetings, and the hotel... and the sex, too," she added with a wicked little grin that made me want to have her all over again right there where we lay. But something stopped me, and I ran my hand along the curve of her face in concern.

"Emily sweetheart, I don't want you to think that me helping you out on the street or at work, was just a ploy to get you into bed. I've wanted you since I saw you; that doesn't mean I've been trying to bribe you into sleeping with me."

"No, no, I know that!" She exclaimed, lashes fluttering over her eyes. "I slept with you because I wanted to. But those are all good things, and you deserve to be thanked."

"Well, in that case, I suppose you're welcome."

"Unless, of course, you're some serial seducer who sleeps with all his interns," she teased, but I could see that there was some genuine curiosity underneath. Emily was a woman who liked to know where she stood, and I respected that.

"No. There have been other women, but no one from

Skyblue. You're the first. And for the record, I still feel terrible that you're my intern."

She settled in against me again, nuzzling her nose against mine. The soft press of her breasts and stomach against me felt outrageously good, and I knew if she kept kissing me and murmuring in that sweet little voice while pushing herself up against me, I would be hard again in no time.

"Well, I'm a consenting adult, so you shouldn't. Although I think it's kind of sexy."

"Oh yeah?" I asked, threading my fingers through her hair. I brushed my thumb across her lips. "Is that why you let me in? Have a thing for older men?"

"Not usually," she giggled. "But it works for you. I guess I've just fulfilled that old stereotype about girls with daddy issues."

I continued to hold her close and stroke her hair. There was a story there, I could feel it, but I didn't want to push her too hard about it. We had been through a lot recently, and she had just exposed herself to me, literally and figuratively, in a big way. But if she wanted to talk, I was willing to listen.

"Is your dad out of the picture?" I asked.

Emily rested her chin on my chest. A cloud had passed over her demeanor, but she was still relaxed and open. I resolved to respect and listen intently to whatever she told me next since it was sure to be something weighty.

"Yeah... He died when I was sixteen. It was really tough for all of us, my mom and my little sister Darlene and I. But I think that out of all of us I was the closest to him. It sounds awful; it's not like he didn't love my mom and Darlene, and I'll bet all teen girls think that about their fathers if they're close... but he was my rock. He was my biggest cheerleader, and he was just so attentive and supportive. I sometimes worry that I might have taken him for granted when he was alive. It's so easy to be selfish when you're that age, you know."

"Oh, baby," I said quietly. I wasn't usually one for endearments with women I had just slept with, especially if I wasn't sure where the relationship stood, but Emily brought it out of me. She was precious, and I wanted her to know that. "You weren't selfish; you were just a kid. Kids lean on their parents; it's what they do. If he was alive, I'm sure what he would want for you is success and happiness."

Emily smiled at me and then gave a little sniffle, and I realized with distress that tears were welling up in her eyes.

"Oh no! Did I say something wrong, are you alright?"

She hid her face in my chest and sniffled again, but now she was laughing. When she looked up, her eyes were still watery, and her face was pink with embarrassment.

"I'm sorry; I'm just emotional! I don't even know why. It's probably the hormones or the endorphins or something."

"It's fine! You're allowed to feel whatever you need to. Come here."

I pulled her back into me, wrapping both of my arms around her. I was never this affectionate with one-night stands, on the rare occasions that I had them. Past girlfriends had complained that my mind wandered back to work when we were in bed together, which was true. But Emily held all my attention at this moment.

"You're not the only one with a complex relationship with their parents," I began, hoping that sharing a bit of my story would make her feel better about sharing her own. "I told you my mom died when I was still in elementary school. My father is still alive, and he's... he does his best to be involved, and he does love my sister and me very much, but he drank a lot when I was in high school. He turned himself around when I was in college, but by then, the damage was done. Sometimes I feel like I grew up without a father. But I told you; that's why people like Aunt Martha were such godsends. That's why I want to make sure that some of the money I make goes back into those neighborhoods, to help out kids like me who need an extra hand."

"I think that's really admirable. New York is an amazing place to live and work, don't get me wrong, but it's... hard. I couldn't imagine having to learn how to navigate it myself when I was just a kid. The New Jersey suburbs weren't exactly glamorous, but they were pretty safe, I guess. I'd still like to live in a neighborhood one day like the one you grew up in. Somewhere where people know each other's families and help each other out if they can."

"There used to be a lot more of it in the boroughs. Now rent prices and gentrification are pushing so many of the old families out and breaking up the local shops. It's really a shame. But I've got this idea for a charity organization that I'm hoping to be able to devote some time to next year, and I hope it can help out."

I was a bit surprised at myself for divulging this so freely. Longtime friends like Olivia and Marcus and Nico knew about my dreams to sow money and volunteer hours back into the neighborhood where I had grown up. Hopefully, through an initiative led by people currently living there so we could be sure we were meeting their current needs. But it wasn't exactly something I chatted about casually. I knew that to many it sounded like a pipe dream or a distraction from my company, but there was something about Emily's openness that told me she would understand or at least would listen to without judgment.

"That sounds like a great idea," she said. "I'm sure people

would really appreciate that. Most people don't visit home after they make it big, and they don't make time to give back."

"I know. I want to try, at least." I ran my hand up Emily's bare back and found that I was actually feeling nervous about this next bit. It wasn't that I hadn't thought it before, but this would be my first time speaking it aloud, even to myself. "You're free to say no, but if you're interested in visiting the old neighborhood with me, maybe there'll be an opportunity after all this crazy press stuff dies down. I've meant to go back anyway to catch up with some old friends, talk to the people on the street about their needs. If you wanted, we could even count it as part of your internship."

Emily's eyebrows shot up, and for an awful moment, I worried I had gone too far. But then a smile burst across her face.

"I would love to! That would be amazing."

I couldn't help but smile too. Her joy was infectious, and my heart beat faster at the thought of spending more time with her, watching her face while she met my friends and family, kissing her on the same front stoop where I had dreamed about building my business empire as a little boy. Maybe I was getting carried away, but I couldn't bother to care.

"It seems like you've made the best of the cards life dealt you."

"It's usually the bad shit that happens to us that makes us into better people as adults. I hope that doesn't sound callous."

"No," Emily mused. "I don't think so. Losing my father was the hardest thing imaginable, but it made me a lot more self-reliant. It made me closer to my mother and sister. I would never choose to live through it again, but it wasn't all bad, in the end.

"You're smart," I said. And then added in a teasing tone, "You know. For a nineteen-year-old."

Emily looked up at me with mischievous electricity in her eyes.

"Oh yeah? I guess that's a compliment coming from an old man."

"Ouch!" I exclaimed with a laugh. "You've got a bad attitude."

"And what are you going to do about it?"

I rolled her over onto her back, and she gave a happy squeal as I pinned her playfully to the bed.

"I'll have to adjust it for you, young lady."

I lost myself in her earnest caresses and breathless laughter for the next half hour and didn't even care when we pulled the fitted sheet off the bed and when she dug her nails into my back hard enough to leave marks.

Eventually, we had to leave the bed. I was reluctant to abandon our self-made Eden, and I kissed Emily's knees as she pulled her socks on and trailed a little line of love bites across her shoulder while I hooked her bra for her. If I didn't have an event to speak at and Sonia to answer to, I would happily stay in here with Emily all night, losing myself to pleasure and studying every line and curve of her body. But as much as she got under my skin, I couldn't let her throw me too far off my goals. Honed focus had been my secret weapon for success until this point, and I couldn't abandon it now.

"Are you nervous about tonight?" Emily asked as I pulled on the shirt I had discarded near her door. She was watching me from her bed with a mix of satisfaction and delight, like watching me get dressed was some exquisite pleasure she had never even imagined.

"Not particularly. Well... Maybe. I don't know. I haven't had a lot of time to prepare for this one."

"But it's all things you're used to talking about right? Sonia said you're just going to give a quick spiel about SkyBlue's mission and what you've got planned for the next decade. Nothing very long."

"Right, just a quick inspirational speech before dinner. The conference just wanted someone in the field to list as a keynote speaker who could draw attendees; they aren't too concerned about what I end up saying."

"It must be nice, though. To be asked."

"Definitely. I would have dropped out if it wasn't important; that's how busy my week has been. But I made a promise, and this is a good conference. So I kept it."

Emily was pulling on her shoes now, and tugging a thick, creamy evening blouse on over her dark jeans. She looked a bit more casual than most of the attendees who would be at dinner, but she would be comfortable enough to wander around taking photographs from any angle she wanted. She looked like a member of my team, like someone who could be seen with me everywhere, and that made me very happy. At that moment, I couldn't imagine traveling without her.

"Do you want to practice your speech with me to get into the zone?"

"That's very sweet, but no. I prefer to stay in my own head the hour or so before a big speaking event. I'm not bad at them, and I don't get stage fright as much as some people do, but they're not my favorite. It's easy for me to lose track of my thoughts or get anxious."

"You should try meditation," she said, packing her camera and lenses away in their little leather satchel. "I do that before I take tests. Always works for me."

"Seriously? You want me to sit cross-legged and chant?"

"No! Meditation doesn't have to be all that. It's just taking a few minutes to clear your head and focus on your breath. Supposedly it makes your concentration sharper and brings down stress levels."

"Well, I could use that," I admitted, running the brush that she handed me through my hair. In the mirror, I managed to assemble myself into someone who did not look like he had spent the last hour ravishing his intern in a hotel bed. "Are you ready to go?"

"Yes," Emily said, clipping some hoops to her ears as she approached me. I was standing by the door, eager to get the speaking event over and done with, but she took an extra moment to stand in front of me and smile dreamily.

"Kiss for luck?" She asked shyly.

I was happy to take her kisses, sweet with the taste of her strawberry lip balm, and almost let them pull me back into bed and away from my responsibilities. But I stayed strong.

"Thank you," I said, pulling away. "Let me walk out first? Just in case Sonia..."

"Oh," she said, voice falling. "Right. I had almost forgotten."

"I know, me too. Just give me a minute and then head out. If she sees something, she sees something. But I'd rather not have that conversation with anyone again."

I gave her one last parting kiss and then ducked out into the hallway, glancing only momentarily to see if Sonia was waiting for me. Luckily, I had beat her there. We still had a few minutes before all of us were supposed to meet and go to the banquet hall together. It looked like I would be spared the awkward conversation about why Emily and I appeared out of her hotel room together.

Sonia arrived a minute later, splashy as ever in a dark emerald blazer and snakeskin shoes. She had pulled her curls up into a forgiving bun, and it looked like she had slept in her makeup.

"Look at you," I said, hoping to distract her from how rumpled my shirt had gotten with a compliment. "I love that color on you."

"Oh, this thing? Thanks; I got it at an estate sale if you can believe it. Where's Emily?"

I shrugged, hoping I looked convincing.

"Still getting her stuff together, I think."

"Did you manage to get any sleep?"

I stiffened a bit, even though I knew tension would just make me more suspicious.

"Ah, no. Too wound up about the speech. You?"

"Slept like the dead. Those beds are heavenly. I'm feeling much better now."

Thank God. If Sonia slept soundly during our few hours of recreational time, there was no way she heard anything, not even through the paper-thin walls of her hotel room.

Emily appeared from her room then, looking a good bit fresher than me. I had the irrational fear that Sonia would know simply from looking at us, from seeing us standing side by side, but she just smiled at Emily as the girl shouldered her camera bag.

"Everyone ready?" Emily asked.

"Sure am," Sonia said, already heading down the hallway. "I'm excited about food. And Luke's speech, of course."

I turned to fall into step behind Sonia, and Emily scurried forward a few steps to catch up with me.

"Your tie," she said, too softly for Sonia to hear, and reached out to adjust it for me. I let her, lingering close while she straightened my disheveled Windsor knot, but it was at that moment Sonia turned a corner ahead of us and caught us out of the corner of our eye. She faltered a bit, doing a double take, and then hurried forward with her eyes on the ground in the hopes that we wouldn't notice that she had seen. But I saw. And my stomach felt like it was full of rocks.

I shot Emily a worried glanced and moved away from her, putting plenty of distance between us. I didn't glance behind me, knowing that if her expression were hurt, I wouldn't be able to handle it. I had to control this situation; I had to give my speech and keep Sonia from jumping to any conclusions, correct or otherwise.

The banquet hall was already packed by the time we arrived, mostly by people in suits milling around with plastic wine glasses or seating themselves at numbered tables and buttering rolls while they waited for dinner to be served. I had been to these kinds of events a hundred times, and they all blurred together. The speech I was going to give about innovation and the future would do nothing to distinguish it any further, but I had a job to do, and I intended to do it.

I lost Emily to the crowd almost immediately as she slipped away to find the best place to take pictures, but I tried not to let my distress show. She was only my intern. Anyone else wouldn't be upset not to have her by his side at all times, and I shouldn't be either. Sonia, reinvigorated from her nap, was great at her job despite any doubts Olivia may have had. She picked the most direct path to lead me through the sea of people to the stage entrance, and she gracefully but firmly turned down people who tried to shake hands with me, pass on business cards, or ask for autographs. If anything, she was even more efficient than Olivia, and no one seemed to argue with a woman in five-inch platform snakeskin stilettos. I made a mental note to bring her as my bouncer for future events.

The backstage space of the banquet hall was as dark and stuffy as they always were, but Sonia managed to keep people from pestering me while I downed bottled water and waited for the conference founder introducing me to take to the stage. My heart was beating at an annoyingly fast pace, out of synch with the calm I was trying to force myself to exude. Isolating myself from noise and stress hadn't helped, so I tried what Emily had suggested. I closed my eyes and breathed deeply, blocking out all other sounds and sensations other than my own breathing. After a minute or so, I no longer had to remind myself to breathe deeply and slowly, and I had managed to put intrusive thoughts and last-minute worries out of my mind.

By the time the founder called my name and invited me on stage to thunderous applause, I was as calm as I had ever been. I could hardly make out any faces in the crowd through the white glare of stage lights, but I knew Emily was out there somewhere, studying my face through her camera lens, and that gave me immense peace. I smiled, unfolded my speech on the podium before me, and leaned into the microphone.

The speech went over better than I could have expected. I held the audience's attention the entire time and even managed to elicit some well-timed laughter. I even felt myself getting a little worked up during this speech. I had given it in some form or another so many times when I got to the part about sowing resources into our future, and into areas of society that needed the most help, I felt surprisingly emotional. By the time I finished my speech, a handful of people were on their feet, and the whole room was clapping and whooping their approval. I beamed down into the crowd, bathed in a rush of elation, and then waved at them before making my way offstage.

Sonia was waiting for me backstage with a smile and my usual afternoon espresso. I didn't know where she got it from, but I was grateful.

"That was amazing! I didn't realize you were such a good public speaker."

"Thank you," I said, taking the coffee. "Where's Emily?"

"Still out on the floor, I think, getting some shots of the banquet hall. I told her we would meet her outside. Come on."

I followed Sonia as she wove a tight trail through the crowded backstage, dodging the people who tried to catch my attention to congratulate me. I had made her promise that this would be as short of a trip as physically possible, and she was delivering on that with great aplomb. We exited the banquet hall through a side door, finding ourselves in the hotel parking lot where Emily waited with a camera in hand, her face reflecting the California sun.

"You did so well!" She exclaimed, blue eyes sparkling like ocean waters. In a moment, Sonia and I were right next to her, and I was looking down into her beaming face, I couldn't help myself. There was no one else around, and Sonia already suspected, so screw it. I knew what I wanted, and I didn't want to pretend like I didn't.

I caught Emily's face in my hands and kissed her, smiling against her lips. I heard Sonia gasp next to me, throwing her hand over her heart, but I wasn't worried about it. She was the least likely person in the whole office to care, as her own love life was usually as complicated and sordid as a soap opera.

Then I heard the unmistakable sound of a camera lens shuttering. I looked up to find that a couple of members of the press had circled the building and were snapping pictures of Emily and me from the corner of the hotel, talking excitedly on cell phones and jotting down the scene on legal pads. All the blood drained from my face.

"So much for keeping things quiet," I muttered.

Chapter Sixteen

EMILY

*L*uke tugged me across the parking lot as fast as my feet could carry me before I even registered what had happened; Sonia ran along behind us with her high heels clacking against the asphalt. The paparazzi had given chase and were hustling along as fast as they could manage, shouting at us to slow down and just answer a few questions, and please, just give us one smile. The world was a blur around me as we ran for the car, blue sky mixing with yellowing California grass and oily gray cement. Eventually, I registered what had happened. Luke had kissed me. In front of Sonia. And now, since the cameras had caught us, in front of the world.

"Let's go hide out in the rooms," Sonia suggested, coming up alongside us. She was already fumbling through her purse for her room key.

"No," Luke snapped. "Do you want them to know where we're staying? Get in the car. We can lose them and circle back later."

All this seemed very extreme to me, but then again, I had never dealt with the rabid attention of the press before. Luke spoke like a drill sergeant leading us through familiar military formations, urging us on towards our own survival. I couldn't imagine living my whole life like this, but now, whether I liked it or not, I was getting just as much attention as Luke.

"Miss, miss!" Someone called behind me. "What's your name? Please miss, will you just tell us what your name is? Are you Luke's girlfriend? Do you work for him? Miss!"

Luke snagged the keys to one of the rental cars from Sonia as we came careening up beside it. She threw herself into the back-seat, and I nearly collapsed into the passenger side, buckling myself in with shaking fingers. Luke was the last to get inside. He shouted something nasty at the press, something I couldn't make out clearly through the windshield, then got into the car and slammed the door. In an instant, the journalists with cameras were pressed up against the vehicle, cameras against the glass snapping intrusive photos. Sonia snarled at them and flipped them off, and I covered my face with my hands, trying to keep from crying. This was all too much.

Luke threw the car into gear and backed up deliberately, narrowly avoiding running anyone over. As soon as he had an opening, he peeled out across the parking lot, hitting thirty-five before we were even on the road. Some journalists had caught wise to his plans and rushed for their cars and news vans, but he was quicker than them. He banked down a side street while they were still navigating the parking lot, and in a few moments, we were lost in the back streets of San Francisco. I didn't think Luke knew where we were going, but he drove with absolute determination.

"I'm so sorry about that," he said, eyes flicking up into the rearview mirror. "Sonia, are you in one piece?"

"Lucky for your dumb ass, I can run in heels," she shot back, righting herself. She had been thrown down onto the floor of the backseat when he took the turn out of the parking lot at a particularly sharp angle. "What the hell kind of PR stunt was that?"

"It wasn't a stunt. I didn't mean to—"

"To what, lock lips with your intern?" She pushed herself up between the seats so she could see my face. "Are you two a thing? Emily, why didn't you tell me? Seriously, how many times have we talked about Mr. Most Wanted over here?"

"What?" Luke said, making a disgruntled face.

"Shut up and drive, Luke. Emily, what the hell is going on?"

"I don't know!" I shot back. I was jumpy and rattled from our close call with the paparazzi. "Things just happened, I—"

"Leave her alone," Luke snapped. "This one is on me. I thought we were alone. I thought you knew. I'm sorry."

"I mean I guessed something had happened between the two of you when I saw her being all sweet on you in the hallway, but I didn't assume that you two would break the Internet."

My throat was dry.

"Break the internet?" I croaked.

In a moment, Sonia had Twitter pulled up on her phone and typed Luke's name into the search bar. Photos of him cradling my face in his hands and kissing me deeply were splashed across the screen with headlines speculating about my identity and our relationship. It was a surreal, out-of-body experience to see myself standing in that parking lot, pushed up on my tiptoes to kiss Luke, while I sat in a car next to him, wishing I could take back the last ten minutes of my life.

"God," I moaned. "I'm going to get fired."

"No, you're not," Luke said. "I own the company. Emily, you're white as a sheet. Are you feeling alright?"

"I feel... I'm a little sick."

"I'm so sorry about this, baby. Lean back and close your eyes if you want to. I'll find us a safe spot to pull over soon."

"Luke, what are you going to do about—" Sonia began, but then stopped when his phone started to buzz insistently.

"Get that," he ordered. "It's in my pocket."

Sonia obediently rummaged around in his pocket until she retrieved his bulky smartphone.

"It's your sister."

"This isn't a good time."

"It could be important. Maybe she saw the pictures."

"Damn it, Sarah... Fine, answer it."

Sonia fumbled with his passcode entry and then pulled the phone to her ear.

"Hello, you've reached Luke Thorpe. This is his assistant Sonia speaking. How may I help you?"

Her chipper office voice was jarring amid our crisis, and I turned around to watch her over my seat. She was biting her manicured nails, face a rictus of distress despite her bright tone.

"Yes... I understand. Of course, yes, I'll let him know..."

Luke glanced over to me from the driver's seat, then switched lanes to get us closer to an easy exit. He seemed to be scoping out businesses and parking lots which would give us the quietest cover to talk and regroup.

"It's probably nothing," he said quietly. "She's probably just trying to get me to go out to dinner with my brother-in-law again."

"She wants to talk to you," Sonia said from the backseat, holding the phone to her chest.

"Tell her I'm busy. She knows better than to call while I'm working."

"Luke, this is important, it's—"

"Sarah always thinks whatever is worrying her at the moment is important; I'll call her back."

"Luke, please shut up and listen to what I'm saying. It's your father. He's had a heart attack."

Luke's jaw tightened, and then the car careened twenty miles over the speed limit off the road and into the parking lot of a Wendy's. He put the car in park in the back near the dumpsters, then passed his hands over his face. He looked gaunt, like he had aged a decade in minutes. Then he took the phone from Sonia, got out of the car, and stood facing away from us, hand squeezing the back of his neck as he talked to his sister.

Sonia and I watched him in silence for a while as he paced, head turned down towards the ground. Then she shook her head and sighed.

"What a bitch of a day. When it rains, it pours."

"Did it sound very serious?" I asked quietly, not daring to glance back at her for fear that there might be bad news written all over her face.

Sonia sagged back against her seat.

"Yeah. She said his brother-in-law rushed his dad to the hospital an hour ago. They don't know all the specifics yet, but it's not looking good."

"God," I breathed. "That's so scary."

Luke nodded now and turned back to the car with a briskness in his step that spoke of purpose. He yanked open the door and leaned inside, still on the phone with his sister.

"Sonia, can you drive? Back to the hotel, please. I need to get my stuff and get to the airport."

Sonia obediently scrambled out and took over driving, pulling smoothly around to the front of the restaurant and then back onto the road. She asked me to navigate for her, and I pulled up the GPS app on my phone while Luke carried on a low, urgent conversation with his sister.

"How long had he been having the pains ...Christ?. No, I didn't know... Since when? Who all is with him there... I know, I know... What hospital did they take him to again?"

He was being as efficient and measured as possible, but I heard the misery in his voice. I remembered what he said last night about his father not being there for him when he needed him, but this wasn't the voice of a man who hated his father. This was the voice of a man who felt responsible for his father, and who was distraught at the idea of not being able to say goodbye to him if it came to that.

Sonia slowed down suddenly as we approached the hotel, moving at a crawl. There was panic in her eyes.

"What's wrong?" I asked.

"We've got no idea if those vultures with the cameras are still there. They're going to be waiting for you, Luke, they know you're staying in the hotel."

"Just a minute, Sarah, just a minute, I'll be right back." Luke pressed the phone to his chest and threw a hard glance out the window. "Well, what are we supposed to do? I need to get my things and get to the airport. Now. Hell, I needed to be there an hour ago, my father is in critical condition, he's—"

"I know. We'll think of something." She gnawed on her lips, and then her eyes lit up with a revelation. "We've got two cars. You two take this one to the airport. Emily, stick with him, make sure he gets where he needs to go and make sure you get back to New York. I'll rush up for our bags and bring them around in another car. I'll make sure they get back to the city; you just focus on your family right now, Luke."

"Thank you," he said, reaching out to squeeze Sonia's shoulder, and then went back to the somber phone call with his sister. They were discussing diagnosis and billing and all sorts of other things I couldn't understand but knew demanded his attention.

Sonia rolled to a stop a couple of blocks away from the hotel and unsnapped her seatbelt, reaching over to squeeze my knee in encouragement before hopping out of the car. I watched as she hustled down the sidewalk in her heels, already rummaging around in her purse for her keys and ID. I knew that she would be alright and that our bags would make it back to New York, somehow. Luke started to slide out of the car, phone wedged between his ear and shoulder, but I stopped him.

"No, stay on the phone with Sarah. I'll drive."

"You'll... Emily, are you sure?"

"I'm sure," I said, already sliding over from my seat into the driver's side. The steering wheel was still warm from Sonia's tight grip, and the keys were already in the ignition waiting for me. My heart was pounding, but the adrenaline of needing to resolve a crisis overshadowed my anxiety about being behind the wheel again. We were only a few minutes away from the airport. Luke needed me to be there for him right now. I could do this.

Luke leaned forward between the seats and kissed me, then disappeared back into the backseat to jot down the address of the hospital from his sister. Moments later, he hung up and was searching for airline tickets on his phone, locating ones that would get us back to the Big Apple the fastest. A few stern phone calls to airlines later and we were booked for a business class flight leaving in fifty minutes.

"Are you sure we can make it?" I worried aloud. My hands were gripping the steering wheel so tightly my knuckles were white. I strained to hear my GPS spout directions over the noise of the road.

"Without bags to check? Absolutely. I'll get us where we need to go, I promise. Thank you for driving."

I tried to smile at him in the rearview mirror, then squealed when a car swerved too close to me.

"Eyes on the road," he said encouragingly, and in a few more minutes we were parked haphazardly in the airport drop-off lane. Luke was out of the car before me and opened the door for me, offering his hand. I took it and let him pull me gently out of the driver's seat onto shaking legs. He spared an extra moment to hug me tightly to his chest, then began to pull me through the bustling airport where we had just been that morning. We were supposed to spend the night in San Francisco and fly back tomorrow afternoon. But plans had changed. In a few hours, the world had changed, and now the press knew all about Luke and I and his father was dying in some hospital bed 3,000 miles away. It seemed like a dream.

As soon as my feet hit solid ground, I let Luke take over. I sagged against him as he returned rental keys, checked us in, helped me slip out of my jacket in the TSA line, located our gate, and led me up the gangplank into our plane. His arm rarely left its secure spot around me, and I was grateful for his fortifying closeness. Some people stared at us and snapped pictures with their camera phones, but neither of us could be bothered to care. It had been a hell of a day already, and it wasn't over, but at least we had each other.

Luke was quiet most of the flight home, lacing and unlacing his fingers as he stared out the window or at his phone, eyebrows pulled together in perpetual dismay. I didn't know enough about the situation to talk him through it, but I did see another way to give him comfort, so I leaned my head against his shoulder and wound my fingers through his. A few days ago, I wouldn't have dreamed that he would allow this closeness and familiarity, but now he kissed the top of my head tenderly and murmured into my hair.

"If he dies, I'll never be able to forgive myself."

"I know. But you didn't do this, Luke. And you're going to him now. You're doing everything you can do."

He nodded, still looking a little haunted, but he squeezed my hand to show that he understood. He rested his head against mine and sighed deeply.

"Thank you, Emily. Thank you for being here."

Chapter Seventeen

LUKE

 ost of that day passed in a blur. I only dimly remember landing in LaGuardia and ushering Emily off the plane. I remember that she insisted on coming with me to the hospital instead of going home to sleep off her day at home. I wanted to insist she get some rest, and under normal circumstances, I would never allow her to involve herself in my family's problems. But she had been through so much already because of me, and I knew she didn't want to be alone. And if I was perfectly honest, going into that hospital and facing the news that my father could be dying, or worse, already dead, made me want to have her by my side. Let the press talk. Let Sarah wonder and let my deadbeat brother-in-law stare. I didn't care. Emily and I needed each other, and I would not deny us that.

Sarah kept me as up-to-date as possible with regular texts, and I was relieved to get off the plane to a flood of messages confirming that my father was unconscious but stable. By the time Emily and I pulled up to the hospital in a taxi, Sarah was texting me my father's room number, letting me know not to expect him to be awake. I told her I brought a friend with me and left it at that. My sister and I might not see eye to eye on many things, but she knew how to leave well enough alone, and she knew I only introduced her to women when I felt ready.

The hospital was no different than any other I had ever set foot in; cold, sterile, and smelling faintly of antiseptics and death. Sarah had already tried to brighten up my father's room with a thin bouquet of cellophane-wrapped flowers bought in from one of the hospital shops, but it didn't do much to improve the atmosphere. My father lay in bed, ashen and motionless and hooked up to machines. A cold feeling settled in my stomach when I realized that I might never see him conscious again, but I put the thought out of my head as quickly as I could.

"It came on so fast," Sarah said. She rushed out to meet us when we arrived and folded both Emily and me into her arms, no questions asked. That was just her way, and I was grateful. "We didn't realize what it was until he started having shortness of breath."

"God," I said. My voice dropped to match her quiet tone as we stood in the room together. We knew my father couldn't hear us, but it seemed right to keep our voices down. "Who caught it?"

"Eric, if you can believe it. He dropped everything and rushed Dad out here right away, no questions asked. I left Ryan with the nanny and came as soon as I could."

I glanced over at Emily. She lingered close by my side, our shoulders touching.

"Eric?" Something inside me gave way, and I sighed heavily. I had spent so many years determined to hate him that I hadn't been able to see the ways he might be good for my family. And now he had done everything he could to save my father's life. I looked over to where Eric was sitting next to my father's bed, looking almost as ashen as he was. Wordlessly, I walked over and pulled him up out of the chair into a tight, one-armed hug. This was the most we had ever touched outside of a perfunctory handshake.

"Thank you," I said, voice thick.

Eric just nodded. He was wiped out from the day, but I knew he understood. We were going to be alright.

The hospital kept my father under close observation for the rest of the day and into the evening. Sarah, Eric and I lingered nearby, sipping cheap hospital coffee and nibbling on Saltines and cookies from the cafeteria, but it was like watching paint dry. Hours passed with no change in status; nurses came and went to check vital signs and pronounce that nothing had gotten better or worse. Soon we were all hungry, tired, and irritable. Emily, in particular, looked like she was going to drop at any moment, so I pulled her out into the hallway for a quiet conversation.

"I appreciate you coming out here with me, but you don't have to stay. You should go home and get some sleep."

Emily wrung her hands, glancing down the narrow, dark hospital hallway. It felt so strange to send her home after our whirlwind day together, but I had a lot to process. Everything had changed around me without warning, and I had no idea how I would go into work on Monday dealing with my father's health, without worrying that there would be questions about the pictures currently circling the Internet. I hadn't looked at my phone since getting to the hospital. I didn't have the stomach for it.

"I'm alright, Luke. Really. If you want me here with you, I'll stay."

My shoulders sagged. Emily had no experience dealing with the press. This was the first day she had probably ever seen the paparazzi up close, much less been pursued by them. She could insist that she was fine all she wanted, but I had seen the terror in her eyes, the confusion, and the shame. The closer she got to me, the more likely the world was going to tear her apart. It would be fun, for a day or two, dating a local celebrity. But I knew that she had been seen too much with me already. If cameras caught us leaving the hospital after my father's heart attack, her world would be irrevocably changed, and not for the better.

I pinched the bridge of my nose and sighed.

"That's very sweet of you, but I... have a lot to think about right now. I'm probably going to go home soon myself and try to sleep."

Part of me wanted to invite her along, to fall asleep in my own bed, holding her body against mine. I wanted to smooth her hair and kiss her gently and feel the rise and fall of her chest, breathing against mine. But that would complicate matters further. I had taken up enough of her time, and she had left enough of a mark on my life for one day.

"Alright," she said softly.

I turned away from her, but she caught my hand and pulled me back in, close to her. Her perfume had faded almost entirely from our insane day, but there was still the faintest hint of vanilla clinging stubbornly to her hair. This nearly broke me. After a brutally long day, I wanted to lose myself in her, to sag into her and thread my fingers through all that hair and breathe her in.

"Luke, can we talk, please?"

"We are talking," I said, eyes searching her face. I felt a substantial conversation coming on, one I wanted to have with her, but my head was pounding from stress and lack of sleep. I needed water and to lie down. It was so hard to think straight with her right in front of me. I didn't even know what time it was, what day it was. I wasn't able to make any decision right now.

"I know you don't need this right now, but over the last couple of weeks... Listen, I know this is all very sudden but we've been through a lot together, and I think it's alright for me to say that I care about you so much. I have feelings for you Luke, I think I might be falling in love with you and I just... don't know what's going on between us."

I felt lightheaded. She had just laid all her cards out on the table in front of me, and I was coming up short of anything to say. I might have felt the same, but I didn't know because there had been no time to think or examine my feelings. I felt like I had passed through the last 24 hours on instinct alone, and this was no time to make big decisions, especially not with my father dying one room away. And not with my reputation potentially in shambles because of a picture with Emily. I didn't even want to think about how this would affect her, or what her school would say to her about the photographs.

"Emily, we've been through a lot together. Emotions have been running high, and I do like you a lot, and I care about your well-being, but I just... don't have the bandwidth to consider anything else right now. You know me. You know my schedule, you know I don't have time for anything committed—"

"That's alright," she said, but her voice was papery and hollow. She had pulled her hands out of mine and put a few inches of distance between us, like a chilly invisible wall. "Thank you for letting me know. I don't know what I was... It's fine. You're right. I should go home."

My heart was heavy as lead in my chest. This was never how I wanted anything to go. I was never supposed to be standing in a dingy hospital hallway in the middle of the night telling the most wonderful woman I had ever met that I didn't have time for her, that I wanted her to leave me alone. But I didn't know what else to do. My father's heart attack drove home the point in painfully real time: life was short. I had a mountain of things I hadn't done yet that I was desperate to accomplish, and I didn't know if there was space in there for a dalliance with my intern, especially when it was threatening to become something more, something all-consuming.

"Alright," I said swallowing. "But Emily, I—"

"Luke?" Sarah asked. She had poked her head out of the hospital room into the dimly lit hallway. Her eyes shined eerily, partially from barely restrained tears, and partly from the fluorescent overhead lighting.

"Hey," I said, glancing over my shoulder. Emily clutched one of her arms, looking down at the floor and nudging at the tile with her shoe. She looked like she wanted to dissolve back into the atmosphere, to be absorbed by the dingy grey walls of the hospital.

"I didn't know where you went," Sarah said quietly. Sheepishly. She was looking at Emily like she didn't know what to do with her, and Emily was folding in on herself. I knew that my sister was a welcoming and warm woman who wouldn't judge Emily or be angry with me for bringing her around, but it had been a long and tiring day. Bringing her along to my father's sickbed had been an impulse decision for my comfort, and now I regretted it. Sarah deserved to grieve in private. Now that the exhaustion caught up with all of us, I could see the desperation in my sister's eyes. She needed comfort. She needed me.

"Is everything alright?" I asked.

"He's still out like a light. It sounded like he was having trouble breathing there for a minute, but everything seems fine now." Sarah moved out into the hallway with us, wringing her hands. "Eric went out to get some more coffee."

"Sarah," I sighed. "It's late. No more coffee, okay? I want you to be able to get some sleep tonight."

"I just can't sleep seeing him like that."

"I know."

I heard a little noise behind me and turned to see Emily shouldering her purse and shuffling a few steps away. I put a hand out to her but stopped myself before I took her hand and drew her back to me.

"Emily, are you—"

"I really should be getting home. Sarah, it was nice to meet you. I'm so sorry about your father, and I hope I haven't been too much of a bother."

"Oh Emily," Sarah said softly, her eyes searching Emily's face. She was disoriented and exhausted, but I could still tell that my sister's nurturing instincts were still active, driving her to comfort this strange young girl who had been swept into my life. I felt torn between the two of them, wanting to support both of them in every way I could but not having the energy for either of them. "It's alright; you don't have to—"

"I've got work on Monday," Emily said, her eyes pleading to be let go. "I should really go."

"I'll call you a cab," I said weakly.

"Thank you," she said, almost inaudibly. A few minutes later, her cab was idling outside, and I was watching her walk away, shoes clacking against the floor as she shouldered her purse and camera bag. She didn't look back.

Sarah wandered out of the hospital room and put her hand on my shoulder, looking into my face.

"Luke," she asked gently. "What's going on?"

I turned to look at her. She looked so delicate in the dim light of the hospital at night, like touching her too hard might bruise her.

"Nothing," I said, voice thick. "Nothing is going on."

Without another word, I enfolded her in my arms and hugged her tightly.

Chapter Eighteen

EMILY

I wasn't sure if Luke was going to show up to work on Monday. He hadn't texted or called for the rest of the weekend, which I mainly spent sleeping off the San Francisco trip, holed up in my room, and watching Netflix with my roommates. Every minute that passed felt surreal, somehow more surreal than the dreamlike hours I had spent wrapped up in Luke's arms. Nothing resonated with me the way it should, not my roommates asking to hear about my trip, or the food I begrudgingly fed myself, or the too-hot emptiness of my bed. I hoped to clear my head and get some things done before heading back to work on Monday, but that just wasn't happening. All I seemed to be good for was moping around, or gnawing anxiously at my fingernails worrying about what I had done or losing myself to heated daydreams of Luke's mouth on my neck. Each of these activities only exacerbated the other two, and soon, I was caught in a miserable loop of regret, heartsickness, and lust.

I tried to flip through the pictures I took on Sunday afternoon to identify some good candidates for marketing materials, but I couldn't do it. One flash of Luke's smiling face up there in front of all those people had me feeling sick to my stomach, so I powered down my camera and stuffed it deep in my bag. I would deal with the pictures, with work, with everything, when I got back into the office on Monday.

I hadn't heard from Sonia since we parted ways in California, but when I arrived at my desk the next morning, I saw my carry-on and makeup bag stacked up neatly next to my desk with a hot pink sticky note attached to them.

You're such a trooper! Sonia had written in a friendly, curling hand that made me want to cry. And then, below it in smaller letters, *congrats on tapping that fine billionaire ass.*

At least Sonia wasn't angry with me or scandalized by my behavior. The rest of the office... who knew? I trusted Olivia not to say anything to anyone in the office, and Sonia had been there and surely realized how much damage a little gossip could cause, but I knew those pictures were circulating the internet. All it would take was for someone to stumble across them and identify me. My face was mostly blocked by Luke's in the few shots I saw. The photos were grainy, tabloid quality, but I still had an awful lot of identifiable red hair.

I managed to make it through about an hour of my workday uninterrupted before Sonia drifted over to my desk, looking guilty, but still runway ready in her white fitted dress with a high Mandarin collar.

"Hey," she said softly. "How are you holding up?"

"Oh, I'm alright," I said and knew I sounded exhausted. Sonia seated herself lightly on the edge of my desk.

"Did you end up going to the hospital with him?" She kept

her voice low, glancing over her shoulder to make sure that the person in the cubicle next to me wasn't eavesdropping.

"Yeah. His dad... wasn't in good shape. We were there for hours, but we still don't know if he's going to pull through or not."

"I was afraid of that. I haven't seen him all morning. He's holed up in his office and won't talk to anyone. He had Olivia cancel all his appointments for the day, I think."

"God," I moaned, putting my head into my hand. "This is all my fault. I was stupid and let myself get carried away and..."

"Oh shut up Em," Sonia said affectionately. "You're just a kid. You fell for someone. He fell back. What were you supposed to do? Say no? I wouldn't have."

"Yeah, well," I grumbled. "I wouldn't be so sure about that whole falling back thing."

"Oh no... Did the DTR moment not go so well?"

"I don't really want to talk about it. Listen, I could barely sleep all weekend thinking about those pictures. Has anyone in the office seen?"

"I don't know honey. I haven't been asking around—"

At that moment, Oliva stood up from her desk, smoothed her skirt, and walked primly over to us. Sonia looked like a child caught with her hand in the cookie jar.

"Oh, hi, Olivia. We were just talking..."

"I know about San Francisco," she said, voice low. She was doing her best to keep her expression neutral, but I could hear the concern in her voice, and maybe a little anger too. "I could kill Luke."

"He told you?" I asked, dismayed.

"No, I just saw..." She glanced nervously over to Sonia. "Does she not know about the pictures?"

"Oh no," I whispered. "Olivia, I'm so sorry, I didn't know anyone was there... we weren't supposed to—"

"I know," She sighed. She looked tired, as if she had been up all night at the hospital too. "Listen, I appreciate the effort, but I didn't have a lot of faith in that whole 'never again' promise the two of you made. People don't work like that."

My shoulders sagged. I felt utterly defeated.

"So everyone knows. The whole office?"

"Not everyone. But I heard a couple of girls talking about it in the lunchroom today. I'm sorry, Emily." I put my face in my hands, feeling miserable. Olivia reached out to touch my arm, a sweet gesture I hadn't expected from her. "If it makes you feel any better, they were all very jealous."

"What are the papers saying?" Sonia asked.

"They don't know who the woman is. Not yet. But I would only give it a few days, tops."

"I can't do this," I said. I felt like I was on a nightmare tilt-a-whirl, screaming for the operator to let me off. There had to be a way out of this. I couldn't sit idly by and listen to the world talk about me, speculate on a relationship I didn't even have, especially when the man who turned my life upside down worked right next door. If Luke and I were going to get through this, we had to have a game plan. I had to know what to say. He had been dealing with the paparazzi far longer than I had and even if he didn't want me in his life, he could at least do the courtesy of helping me out of the mess he had gotten me into.

I was on my feet before I knew I was standing, Sonia looking at me with mouth agape.

"Don't even think about it," Olivia said, but we both knew she couldn't stop me. I had come to work that morning bare-faced, barely taking the time to swipe some moisturizing sunscreen and mascara onto my face before running out the door. Now I rummaged around in the makeup bag rescued from a San Francisco hotel room and swiped on my favorite peach lipstick. It didn't do much to make me look put-together, but it made me feel more like myself.

Before either of the other women could stop me, I was marching down the hallway towards Luke's office. I felt more eyes following me than usual and caught snatches of a couple of whispers as I walked by. People were talking, and I knew gossip spread like wildfire. It was already too late to save my secrets, but I still might be able to salvage my reputation.

I knocked three times before letting myself into Luke's office, not waiting for his reply. I thought by now we were close enough that I could request an audience with him whenever I wanted. At least that seemed fair to me at the time. He was on the phone when I entered, and he looked startled to see me at first. Then the expression faded into neutral tiredness, and he gestured silently at a nearby chair for me to sit down like I was a low-ranking employee waiting for my meeting with him. I obeyed, cheeks burning as I waited for his attention.

"Thank you... Yes that all sounds fine to me, you know I trust you with all this... Of course. Listen, I've got someone here right now, can I call you back?... Sure. I appreciate it. Bye."

He set the phone down with a definitive click and turned, his hands on his hips. He looked his age then, or well past it, the lines around his eyes made more prominent by exhaustion and, as I realized with horror, grief.

"Emily. What is it?"

His voice was soft but flat, entirely devoid of the sweetness that he had lavished on me in San Francisco. This was a man with absolutely nothing left to give.

I had gone in there with requests to make, answers to demand. I was bound and determined to elicit his help in fixing this problem we had gotten into together. But now, all I could manage was a miserable, "Luke."

"My father passed away this morning," he said. "Congestive heart failure. That was Sarah, calling about the funeral."

Tears stung my eyes on his behalf. I had never met his father, but I couldn't imagine anything more miserable than losing a parent. After all, I had done this once before.

"I'm so sorry," I breathed.

"What do you need, Emily?" He asked.

"I..." I didn't know what I wanted now. Any request would be ill-timed and completely irresponsible, but he was pinning me in place with those green eyes that once looked on me kindly. Now they were hard and wary. "The newspapers..."

"I know. I'm so sorry you've been caught up in all this. But it will blow over soon, I promise. I'm completely willing to deny that the girl in the pictures is you. I'll just make up some old girl-friend, and it will be over."

This wasn't what I wanted to hear. I wanted to work through this together, as a team, with a unified plan that would bring us closer together. Now, he was just pushing me further away.

"Luke," I said, trying to begin this whole conversation again. "I'm not mad at you. I'm just worried. I don't know what's going on out there or between us."

"Nothing's going on anywhere," he said tiredly. "I told you."

That hurt, and I couldn't help the fresh tears that welled up hot in my eyes. I tightened my jaw, begging them not to fall, and Luke pinched the bridge of his nose. He looked like a king who had lost his entire empire in one day.

"You're not in trouble, Emily. I'm going to do everything I can to protect you from harm. You're going to be alright."

"But you're not alright. Your father—"

"This is something I need to handle myself. Please. This is a family issue, and I shouldn't have brought you along with me to the hospital, it was asking too much. There's so much to do for the funeral and I just... I don't have room for anything else. I'm sorry."

I had always thought love songs that whined about having one's heart broken into pieces were too dramatic, but now I felt a pang in my chest like something splitting right down the middle. I had been stupid to come. I had been stupid to believe I had anything to offer him or was owed any of his time.

"I understand," I said, rising to my feet. Luke was watching me with a tight expression, his hands bunched into fists at his sides. For all I knew he might have wanted to go with me, but he made it clear that ship had sailed. "I'm sorry for taking up so much of your time, Mr. Thorpe."

"Emily..." He began, but I didn't let him finish. I marched back to my desk, letting his door swing shut behind me, and ignored the scandalized glances that followed me. People pulled out their phones to text the latest gossip or leaned over to let their cubicle mates know they had seen me coming out of his office, but I didn't let myself care. None of them mattered, not even Luke mattered right now. Only I did. So I sat down at my desk and put in the best damn eight hours of work I have ever logged in my life and ignored the persistent pain in my chest.

Chapter Nineteen

LUKE

*Y*ou never expect how much work it takes to plan a funeral until you're in the middle of planning one. My father had not left behind clear end-of-life wishes for his children, which made an already complicated situation stickier. Everyone had a different idea of how things were to be handled but in the end I ended up conceding most of the responsibility to my sister, who rose to the occasion with the grace of a saint. I spent most of Monday on and off the phone with her, the hospital, my lawyers, the funeral directors. Everyone needed something different from me, wanted more money or opinions or more of my limited time. The day passed in a miserable blur, and I never left my office once. When Olivia came in with my coffee, I just shook my head at her and sent her away with an apology in my eyes. Today, I didn't want friends. I didn't even want to exist.

I knew I could have handled things better with Emily. Every hour her crushed expression would come back to mind, tormenting me, but the pain was dulled by my exhaustion and grief. The few hours of bliss I had shared with Emily were overshadowed by the knowledge that at that time, my father had been falling ill all the way across the country, and I hadn't been able to move quickly enough to get back in time to say goodbye. The last time we spoke I had brushed him off, ever the ungrateful, bitter child. Now I would never have a chance to make good on my promise to get dinner with him and the rest of the family.

I actually left work at a decent hour that day and traveled to Sarah's townhouse, where Aunt Martha was sitting with my sister and sipping coffee in the living room. When she saw me she stood without a word and folded me into her arms. She smelled like home, and I almost broke down crying for the first time since I had heard about my father's death.

"I am so, so sorry, Luke," she said. "It should never have to be like this, a child burying their parent. But please don't blame yourself."

"I wasn't there," I said into her shoulder, voice muffled by her. "I was working too much, I should have been home, I should have..."

"We cannot live our lives in shoulds," she said firmly, "And I won't have you carrying this guilt around for the rest of your life. Let it go, son."

Sarah watched on from the couch, crying softly but persistently. She had always been the crier in the family and I was sure her eyes hadn't been dry for days. I reached out to her and pulled her into the hug, and she buried her face in Martha's shoulders and cried and cried until she was spent.

While we were still embracing, Ryan appeared down the hallway, looking rumpled and wide-eyed. He didn't seem like he got much sleep recently either, and I wondered if anxiety for all the grown-ups around him, or the absence of his grandfather had been keeping him up.

"Uncle Luke?" He asked.

Sarah held out her hand to him and he joined our family hug, letting me smooth back his hair from his brow. After a moment I pulled away from everyone, but scooped Ryan up like I had when he was a baby and settled him down next to me on Sarah's couch. I felt totally exhausted, like I hadn't slept in a year, but I knew that this was just the beginning of the stress. There would be funeral arrangements soon, and the reading of the will and the statements in the papers and all the socializing I was going to have to do with relatives I hadn't seen in ages.

"Where's Eric?" I asked, realizing suddenly that Sarah's husband wasn't in the house with us.

"He's down at the funeral home talking to the director, getting quotes and looking over different funeral packages. I just... I couldn't do it, Luke."

"Of course not. I understand."

"It was so sweet of him to go but I feel bad sending him off alone. He's been such a rock through all this."

"I know," I murmured, making room for Ryan as he snuggled up next to me. He set his head down in my lap, looking miserable. All the usual color was gone from his cheeks, and I thought it horribly unfair that someone so young should have to experience all this death and stress. Adults were supposed to have everything figured out, they were supposed to be able to handle these sorts of things behind closed doors without children seeing them, but we weren't able to. We were hardly able to figure things out over the phone, Sarah and Aunt Martha and I, much less come to a total consensus. My father had never liked talking about death, and he hadn't planned for it. That, as it turned out, was making our lives a lot harder than expected. The only one of us who knew anything about funerals was Aunt Martha, who had already buried both of her parents.

We ended up leaning heavily on her expertise the next couple of days, and I stayed with everyone in Sarah's townhouse in the Upper East Side. She had done well for herself with her marriage to Eric, and I had made sure she never wanted for anything until then, so she had plenty of room to spare. Aunt Martha was good enough to spend the next few afternoons with us, going over paperwork at the kitchen table with Sarah while I cooked up a grilled cheese for Ryan or played checkers with him in the living room. I think Sarah was grateful to have someone help ease the stress of parenting while she processed our father's death.

Eric continued going in to work, but as soon as he stepped into the house in the evening he became fully available to his wife and child, pulling them into his arms and asking, with real gravity, how they were and if there was anything he could do. My respect for him grew tenfold during the couple of days I spent living with him in my sister's house, and by the end of my visit we had reached a grudging peace.

The third evening, after Ryan had taken his shower and been tucked into bed by Sarah and me, we stood in the kitchen with Eric sharing a bottle of red wine. It was the first real socializing we had done during my time there, since most of our waking hours were devoted to Ryan, or funeral planning, or to my answering work emails from my phone. For the first time in, well, ever, we were all relaxed. Eric was telling some story about work that wasn't absolutely humorless, and it was making Sarah laugh, which was making me smile. I realized that I was relaxed, leaning against the kitchen counter with wine in my hand and my elbow brushing against my sister's, and that's how I knew it was time to go home. It was time to pull myself back up and get back to daily life.

"Luke, can I get you more wine?" Eric asked, reaching for the bottle.

"No, thanks."

"I'll take some," Sarah said, putting out her glass. She had a lovely flush in her cheeks from the wine and the laughter and it was the first time, I thought, I had seen her genuinely happy since our father's death.

"You wouldn't believe some of these guys at work," Eric went on. "Or maybe you would, Luke. I hear SkyBlue attracts all sorts of eccentric Silicon Valley types."

"Some," I admitted. "But most of them aren't so bad."

It was impossible to keep Emily, glowing-eyed and happily exhausted in bed next to me, out of my mind. Somehow, even through the haze of grief, I had been seeing her for days, while I was awake and in my dreams. Guilt rose up in my throat whenever I thought of her, but it seemed too late now to reach back out. She didn't want a part of this, anyway. She deserved better than someone who only knew how to work and could barely grieve his own father properly because he had lost touch with his own family.

"Listen," I said, swirling my wine around in my glass. "I think it's about time for me to go back to work."

"So soon?" Sarah asked, looking a little distressed. But Eric didn't seem upset. He just nodded at me, man-to-man, indicating that he understood perfectly. Sometimes, the best way to deal with your life getting turned upside down was to continue on with your daily routine as though nothing had changed and to let the work bring healing.

"It's been three days, Sarah. As wonderful as it is to spend time with you both and with Ryan, I can't hide out here forever. I have a company to run."

"Aw, Luke." Sarah leaned her drowsy head against my shoulder, threading her arm through mine. "It's been so nice to see you."

"It's been good to see you too. I think I'm going to get my things and head back to the apartment this evening, try to get a good night's sleep in my own bed before work tomorrow. I've got a company to run."

"I know," she said, and pushed up on her tiptoes to kiss my cheek. Eric put out his hand and gave me a firm, heartfelt handshake.

"Damn good to see you again, Luke. Listen. I've been meaning to apologize. For that dick move with the investments and SkyBlue. I shouldn't have pulled out at the last minute like that; I was a stupid kid and I should have kept my word—"

"Eric."

I took his shoulder in my hand and gave a reassuring squeeze. "It's alright, really. We're alright."

Sarah's eyes shined with joy and Eric nodded at me. We were going to be fine. All of us, together, if we could just get through this funeral. But that, I knew, was a bridge I would have to cross in the coming week. Until then, I had a company to run and a public image to rehab from the gossip mills.

It was going to be a long week.

Chapter Twenty

EMILY

*L*uke arrived quietly back to work, with no public announcement. It was only remarkable because no one at SkyBlue remembered when he had taken personal time away from the office before, but his father had just died. If that didn't make you step back and take stock of your life, nothing would.

The gossip hadn't stopped in the days that Luke had been gone, but it had gotten better. Some girls at work threw me knowing, eyebrow-waggling glances in the lunchroom, and one outright asked me if I was seeing Luke and if he was any good in bed. Plenty of people didn't seem to care either way, though, and others didn't seem to have seen the photographs at all. I hadn't gotten any strongly worded emails from my school either and after a while my fear of opening my phone to find that they had fired me dissipated. Things slowly returned to normal.

Well, most things. Things between Luke and I were not normal, or at least I felt like they weren't. We hadn't even had time to find our equilibrium before we were wrenched apart, but maybe that was all for the best. Still, that pain in my chest came back every time I thought about it, and sometimes I would just start crying in the shower or on the subway for no good reason. I felt cheated out of what could have been the best thing to ever happen to me. I thought about calling my mother maybe ten times, but each time I chickened out and put the phone down. I didn't want to have to explain myself to her, and I was so afraid she was going to be disappointed with me after the little speech she gave me about keeping it professional with my coworkers.

I ended up breaking down on a Thursday afternoon when I overheard Olivia talking to Sonia about Luke's schedule in the lunchroom.

"He'll be out of the office tomorrow," she said. She was looking a little better than she had the week prior, with her hair swept back into an elegant chignon and her face immaculately made up, but she still seemed tired, like she needed a whole week away from the demands of work to recharge. People always looked at the insanely high workload and output of SkyBlue and immediately thought of Luke, but Olivia took on just as much as him, and she also took on his well-being. "But if you leave the paperwork with me, I can get it approved first thing next week."

"I appreciate it. Where's he going to be again? Another speaking thing?"

I stiffened a bit where I was standing next to the electric kettle and nearly splashed hot water out of my mug and onto my feet. I did my best not to show my surprise and snagged a paper towel from the rack to mop up the tiny puddle I made. My hands were shaking.

"Near Long Island, yeah," Olivia went on. "Some tech incubator event, I can't keep it all straight."

They noticed my presence then, maybe just from the waves of anxiety and grief I was radiating. Oliva ducked her head in guilt, worrying at her fingernail with her teeth as though that could hide what she knew, and what she had just let spill in front of me. Sonia gave me a sympathetic smile, but it was too late. I knew.

Luke had been invited to speak at another event and he hadn't invited me along as his photographer. I don't know what I expected, since our last session had ended so catastrophically and the photos from San Francisco were still languishing on the memory card of my Nikon, but it stung all the same.

I rushed out of the kitchen before either woman could see my tears or try to pull me into conversation, then I swept my personal items into my purse from my desk and clocked out early. I needed my mother, and my sister. I was a grown woman and should be able to handle this by myself, and I should have listened when my mom took the phone away from Darlene and told me to watch my back and my heart while I was on the job. But I couldn't do this alone anymore.

My mother looked genuinely surprised when she opened her front door to find me standing on her stoop. I didn't know if she would be working at the hotel or if Darlene would even be home from art club. Mom had been taking on more and more hours at the hotel since my father died, especially with Darlene becoming more independent as she grew older. I knew that we all had our ways of escaping from the pain of my dad's passing: my mother overworked, Darlene threw herself into her hobbies and I... well, I had just followed the plan my father and I had laid out for me to the letter, except for the part where I fell into bed with a man thirteen years older than me and nearly ruined both our careers in the process. Now I had come full circle and was standing with a tear-streaked face in front of my childhood home, the home where I had grown up and where my father and I had discussed so many of his dreams for me. I was sure that in the wildest stretch of his imagination he had never considered this.

"Mom," I said hoarsely, even though I promised myself I would explain myself rationally, and I had promised myself I wouldn't cry. I was terrified of being scolded, so worried that she would hear about the trouble I had gotten into and give me a piece of her mind, and chide me for skipping out on work while she was at it.

But my mother looked down at me with the softest, most concerned look in her eyes.

"Bunny? Are you alright?"

I burst into tears on the spot, and my mother enfolded me in her arms and pulled me into the house without question. Everything was just as I remembered it; the slightly cramped seventies style entryway, the open kitchen and living room/den combo stuffed with beaten-up couches, cozy leather armchairs, and the flat screen TV my father had insisted we couldn't live without. The living room had been his realm when he was still alive, subject to his questionable decorating taste, but no one in the family had the heart to redecorate after he died. As a matter of fact, I realized that my mother had changed almost nothing in the house since he died, certainly not the rooms he spent the most time in, and I wondered if we all were just trying to go on like he had never left us, like he had just stepped out for a six pack of cola and some ice and would be back in time for dinner.

Darlene was already in the living room, curled up in an armchair with her tablet resting on her knee. She was a better artist than I had ever been even though she couldn't take a picture to save her life, and as she had grown, coloring books had given way to sketch pads and paint canvases and electronic tablets where she could draw and shape and stipple to her heart's content. My mother could complain about her antisocial habits all she wanted, but we both knew that art was Darlene's most precious and valuable outlet, the thing that kept her from completely losing it when my dad died. It was hard enough to be a teenage girl without a death in the family, and if spending hours a day hunched over her tablet, stylus pen in hand, was what made her feel complete and balanced, so be it.

"Em!" Darlene exclaimed. "Since when were you supposed to come to visit?"

"Since now," I said miserably, sinking down onto the lumpy cushions that I had bounced on as a toddler and curled up on with friends for middle school ice cream and pizza-filled movie marathons. Just being back in this house made me want to keep crying and never stop.

My mother drifted into the living room after me, looking mildly distraught in her pressed grey denim shirt and jeans with her hair tied up in a handkerchief. If I had to guess, I would say I caught her in the middle of one of her cleaning sprees, which was usually how she spent the few days she had off work. I could practically see her fluttering around the house with a mop and a feather duster, doing her damndest to get Darlene to help out or vacuuming under her chair while she drew and sulked. It was a familiar scene, one that I had spent my high school days wedged right in the middle of, scrubbing dishes or getting distracted while "cleaning" my room by all the beloved old books I found. It was how we spent many of our days off together, filling our time with chores so we didn't have to spend too much time talking to each other. It wasn't that we didn't like each other. It was just that we had virtually nothing in common and therefore, not much to talk about outside of the half hour we spent having a family dinner every night at six pm on the dot, because my mother insisted, and because it had been my father's favorite ritual.

Now my mother came to sit beside me and covered my hand with her own. She smelled like citrus all-purpose cleaner, and face powder, and fresh laundry.

"What's wrong, sweetheart? You look like you've been through hell and back."

"I feel that way," I said. Then I realized that I might alarm her more than was entirely necessary. "I'm okay, though! I'm in one piece. No eviction notice or lost job or broken bones just..."

"A broken heart?" My mother hazarded.

This broke down the last few walls I had against letting her in. I told them both everything. About the carjacking, about Luke, about the job and all the after-hours meetings I had been pulled into. And did it sitting on the couch, crying into a napkin my mother had pulled out of her pocket. Darlene, to her credit, was a good listener. She didn't roll her eyes or interject herself, and she occasionally glanced up from her tablet to take in more of my story.

"This is so wild," she said when I paused for breath. "I can't believe you seriously were running around with the CEO of your company, boinking after hours."

"Darlene!" My mother said firmly. "Don't be crass."

"She just told us she did!"

"Darlene I could use a little support right now," I said, my face hot and swollen from crying. I was so tired of crying and was ready to not shed another tear for the rest of the year. Darlene made an irritated noise and went back to shading in some contour on the face of whatever celebrity or book character she was drawing. Darlene would get fixated on faces, or hands or silhouettes, and draw them again and again until she got them perfectly right. Her room was a weird assemblage of body parts hanging from the walls, printed on glossy print paper or sketched hastily onto napkins, notebook paper, or graph paper. She collected more body parts than your average serial killer, I thought.

"Emily," my mother began carefully, setting down her glass of iced tea on the living room table. She had insisted on bringing out tea for us all while I told my story, maybe because she thought it would make me feel better. Probably so she would have something to do with her hands. She always had something in the fridge ready to offer guests because she had long ago found it would prevent them from loitering in the entryway, unsure of what to say.

"I'm so sorry you're upset but this... I just never expected you to get caught up in something like this. Now I'm not judging you—"

"I'm feeling judged."

"Welcome to my world," Darlene muttered.

"Just listen to me," my mother went on. "You know how important this internship is to you and I'm sure that man is charming and good looking and all sorts of things but... you know this constitutes a violation of ethics, right? You could get in big trouble for this. And God, those pictures..."

"He was the one who kissed me, how was I supposed to know that there were cameras all around?"

"You take pictures for a living, Bunny, I'm sure you could have figured it out."

I immediately regretted telling her about the photographs, but I didn't know how to drive home the severity of what had happened without revealing them. Darlene had done me the courtesy of pretending like she hadn't seen the photos when I brought them up. She even raised her eyebrows in mock surprise, but I had seen her scrolling through her phone moments before, probably flipping back through snapshots of the evidence exchanged with friends. I didn't blame her. If something had caught my sister locking lips with one of the most eligible bachelors in New York City, I would want first dibs on that gossip too. I'm sure it was one of the most interesting things to happen to anyone she knew in this sleepy New Jersey suburb where nothing ever happened except for the occasional convenience store robbery or local investment banker going to jail for embezzling company funds. We seemed to have a lot of those in our neighborhood, and the occasional trials had livened up long, boring summers between my long, boring school years.

"I won't let myself feel bad for just existing in public. Who do those people think they are, anyway? Poking their nose in private business between two consenting adults. He should sue them."

"Luke's a public figure. When you get as famous as he is, there isn't any private life anymore. Come on Emily, you should know this. Didn't you take all those communications law and media relations classes your first year? How is it that I know more about libel than you?"

"I know what libel is, Mom, and I know this isn't it. I was just being dramatic."

As good as it was to be back home being doted on by my mother, there were part of her attentions that I would have been just fine without. No matter how much she tried to frame it as something else, her worrying did feel judgmental, like she had never made a mistake in her youth that she could remember now.

"I'm trying to do the right thing," I groaned. "But I'm so miserable in that office now. I'm just counting down the days until this internship is over, I want to quit, I want to do something else."

"If you quit, you'll have to find another summer internship and there's no way that's happening," Darlene said, brutally honest as ever. "Especially if you can't get a good letter of rec from someone at that company. Sorry sis."

"Think of your future," my mother urged. "Think of Paris. You have to be more responsible."

"I am thinking of my future! I just don't know how to—"

My phone vibrated insistently on the table, and I snatched it up in irritation. A worried phone call from Joanna or a snippy email reminder to register for my fall classes was the last thing I wanted right now, and I had half a mind to snap at whoever was unlucky enough to catch me in this mood.

To my shock, it was Olivia. All the anger melted out of my system, replaced by pure unbridled terror. Oh God, what could she want? Had she found out something more? I felt so very, very tired.

I wiped the tears from my face and stood, already moving into the hallway. Privacy. I needed privacy.

"I'm sorry, I need to take this, just one minute..."

"Bunny, who is it?"

"Just a sec, Mom, please, I just need to—"

"Let her go," Darlene said. "Maybe it's the guy."

I lingered in the half-darkened hallway and put the phone to my ear, asking quietly,

"Hello?"

"Emily, it's Olivia."

Her voice sounded weighted on the other end. I knew she must have spent the last few hours at the funeral, one of the few people in Luke's inner circle to be invited.

"Is something wrong?" I asked immediately.

"Don't worry, this isn't about work. Can I talk to you for a few minutes? Are you alone?"

I glanced over my shoulder at my mother and Darlene, still murmuring among themselves in the hallway.

"Sure, one minute."

Moving by instinct in the dark, I let myself into my child-hood bedroom, long-since renovated into a combination home office and guest bedroom. I sagged down onto the creaking mattress, feeling like I couldn't trust my legs.

"Go ahead."

"I'm sure the last week has been hell for you. How have you been?"

I wasn't expecting this personal line of questioning, or the softness in her voice when she led me down it.

"Oh, um... I'm hanging in there. It's alright. Surreal, but alright. No one at work has been awful to me or anything so that's good. My, um, my family did find out. So that was a conversation."

"I'm sure. Are you with them now?"

"Yes."

"Good. I'm glad you were able to get out of the city and take a break. Listen, I want to talk to you about Luke."

My throat tightened instinctively. I was sure that Olivia had found time to question him about us, probably to agree with him that I was a bad influence and a distraction that should be kept out his life. Maybe this was the call to put me in my place, to drive home the fact that I was not welcome in his life.

"Okay, I'm listening."

"I've known Luke since we were kids, barely eighteen together at college. He's always been incredibly dedicated to his passions and to the people he cares about, and I've been lucky enough to be in that sphere for some time now. I know him just as well as Carl or anyone else. And I know what his patterns are like."

I swallowed hard. I didn't think I could handle hearing about all the other girls Luke had bedded and dropped in a fit of stress, if that's where this conversation was going.

"Luke is... He's a very intelligent man, but he's stupid where it counts. Do you know what I'm trying to tell you?"

"Not really," I admitted.

Olivia sighed on the other end, and I realized she must be pacing a room. Was she still at the funeral, maybe tucked into some private chamber of the funeral home?

"Luke's gut instinct when something goes wrong is to withdraw and bury himself in his work. He's like an emu. I've seen him wreck friendships doing that and alienate his own family. I knew it was only a matter of time before some poor girl got caught in the crossfire, and I'm sorry it had to be you."

"Oh. Well. Thank you, I guess."

"I've been with him all day. I don't have to tell you he's really fucked up about his dad, but you know he'll never admit that. I've been with him all day. I can tell he feels rotten about how things ended with you, and when I tried to ask him about it he looked so miserable you would have thought I kicked his puppy. He would never admit this to you himself, and he would be furious with me for saying so... but he cares about you, Emily. That's so glaringly obvious to everyone else. And he needs you."

My heart fluttered in my chest, and I thought it might burst right then and there from shock and excitement.

"Are you serious?" I breathed. "But he said—"

"I know what he said. Luke's an emotionally repressed dumbass, but he's getting better. And no one is very emotionally articulate when they're staring down deadlines and planning a funeral."

"I guess that's true."

"Listen, I'm not going to tell you to come out here. Everyone's had a long day but if you still were interested in him and you felt up to it—"

"Definitely," I said, before she had even finished. "Yes."

"I hoped you would say that."

"But I thought... That you didn't approve of... Well, Luke and I."

Olivia sighed on the other end and for a moment there was silence. My heart hammered in my chest. I was terrified that I had offended her, or had invited her to have second thoughts.

"I'm not overly fond of workplace romances myself but I know that sometimes, you just meet someone and it happens. I didn't know where this was going at first or what it was going to do to Luke, but now I see that you're a net positive in his life. And he could take very good care of you, Emily. He's incredibly attentive and generous when he's found someone he likes. I think I'd like to see that for both of you."

I felt like I was going to cry all over again.

"I appreciate that very much."

"I'm glad. He'll be at that incubator event in Long Island

giving a speech tomorrow but if you wanted to come by his office on Monday morning, I wouldn't stop you."

"Thank you," I said, mind racing. I was already up on my feet, moving back down the hallway. "I'll see you on Monday. Seriously, thank you."

"Who was that?" My mother asked when I arrived back into the living room. At once, I gathered up my belongings.

"It was someone from work. Listen, it's... kind of an emergency. I have to go, I'm sorry."

"But you just got here! I thought you were going to spend the night."

"I know, I'm so sorry. Thank you for listening Mama, really." I stooped down to kiss her cheek. She was still sitting on the couch, looking stunned. "You're the greatest. I'll come back and we'll do a nice dinner soon. I just... I have to handle this. Darlene—"

"Go on," she said, flapping her hand at me. She was already half turned back to her art tablet. She did, however, spare a moment to shoot me a wink as I yanked open the door. "Go and handle your business. And call me later!"

Chapter Twenty-One

LUKE

I hadn't wanted to go to Long Island, not for the incubator event or any other reason. But for some reason, I was still standing in the tiny, cramped green room of a startup co-working space, drinking bottled water while I sweated in the shoddy air conditioning. This had been one of the rash of events I had agreed to during my first week back after my father died when I was almost manic with focus to compensate for the gaping hole inside my chest. It was a hole where my father, my sense of purpose, and Emily all would have fit with room left to spare, and the longer I tried to ignore it, the larger it seemed to grow. Now it ached dully inside my chest like an old bullet wound that would act up from time to time for the rest of my life. Needless to say, I wasn't feeling very confident about this speech.

I tried to remember what Emily had told me about breathing and synching my mind to the sensation of air traveling in and out of my lungs, but every time I closed my eyes all I saw was her face, her eyes sparkling as she laughed or her beautiful mouth open with pleasure. There was no escaping her or how nauseous I felt when I thought about our last conversation. I sent her away, and she left me without looking back, without even saying another word to me. It had seemed like the right thing to do at the time. Now it just seemed like another bad idea in a long line of poor choices that were coming back to haunt me.

But there was nothing to do about that now. I went on in five minutes, and I would have to give the same speech I had given in San Francisco as though it were brand new, as though it were the best speech I had ever given and not a reminder of my disastrous trip with Emily and Sonia. But I had promised an old friend that I would speak to his small group of rapt tech students and startup entrepreneurs, hand-picked from the best their fields had to offer. It was an event I should have felt enthusiastic about, an opportunity to connect with and inspire the next generation of innovators. But all I felt was hollowness.

I took to the stage in a wash of white-yellow light and with a smattering of light, polite applause. I knew the speech so well I shouldn't have to look down at the printout I had brought along, but I kept glancing down to make sure I was on the right track, placing the proper emphasis on the message I wanted to drive home. More than once, I trailed off, struggling to regain my control of the room. Nothing felt right. I was entirely off my game, devoid of the charm that had gotten me this far in life. I felt miserable. I didn't want to be here. I wanted to be at my desk, or dinner with my father, or in bed wrapped around a woman who loved me. Anywhere but here.

Then I looked out into the audience and saw her.

Emily was sitting in the third row, looking for all the world like another student participating in the startup meeting. A blazer was thrown on over her T-shirt, and her long red hair pulled up into a ponytail. I almost abandoned the speech entirely when I saw her, but then she met my eyes and smiled and gave me a little nod to show that she was listening and yes, that she was there for me. I couldn't believe it. I had no idea how she came to be here, presenting herself so perfectly with a notebook in her lap and her camera in her hand, but I suspected Olivia had something to do with it. I wanted to be angry with her for violating my privacy and giving out my schedule, but I just couldn't be. Not with Emily sitting here so close to me.

I got through the speech quickly after that, and to my great surprise, with a fair bit of mastery. I felt more at ease with her there, and newfound confidence flowed through my veins that infused my words with fire and charisma. The students gathered murmured their approval among themselves, and some snapped pictures on their smartphones or scribbled down quotes they thought were particularly apt. By the end, I had everyone in the room eating out of my palm, and hands were shooting into the air with insistent questions.

I tried to escape the podium without getting mobbed by students, but that wasn't easy. Everyone had a question that just couldn't wait, or wanted an autograph or a picture with me. I tried to appease everyone, but my eyes couldn't stop searching the room for Emily. When I finally saw her, trying to press towards me in a swirl of black linen and white silk, I reached out my hand and grabbed her. This time, I knew I wouldn't be letting her go. Not now, and not ever.

I tugged her towards me by the wrist, and my heart twisted when the corners of her perfect mouth turned up in a coy smile. Her cheeks were round apples, and her eyes gleamed with interest as I stood in front of her, effectively ignoring the world around us. People jostled closer or said my name, trying to catch my attention for a quick question about whatever research they were working on, but I didn't care. All I cared about was Emily and the warmth of her hand in mine.

"I didn't know you were coming," I said.

"Olivia told me you might be down here. She said... Well, she said a lot of things."

"I'm sure she did," I said, marveling at Emily. I couldn't believe she was here, standing in front of me and smiling like I hadn't been a colossal dick to her the last time we spoke, like she actually wanted to see me again. "I'm so sorry about San Francisco, and the way I acted after. I was overwhelmed, and I shut down, but that's no excuse. You deserve better than that, Emily."

"I forgive you," she said softly. "None of us were at our best that day. You were only doing what you thought was right."

"Yes, well, I was wrong. You're one of the best things that have happened to me in a long time, and I should never have pushed you away. As a matter of fact, I'd like to get to know you much better, properly this time, with a dinner date and a chauffeured car and the whole nine yards."

I didn't care that we were surrounded by people and that everyone could hear. I wanted them to know, I wanted this to be real, and I wanted Emily to know how much I valued her.

"I think that sounds nice," she said, sidling closer to me.

"You think so? You think I can kiss you while I'm at it?"

"I think I'll let you."

I tilted her face up with my hand on her chin delicately and kissed her like it was the last time I would ever do it, like it was the first time, like it was the only kiss of my entire life. We ignored the hoots and the camera flashes and the excited squeals from everyone around us. At that moment, only the two of us existed. And I, for one, was grateful for the second chance.

EPILOGUE

*P*aris in the fall was more beautiful than anything I ever imagined. The mild rain left a veneer of shine on everything, from the cars to the streets to the grand old buildings, and I spent most of my days wandering through the city with my camera in hand, documenting every pigeon and streetlamp and sticky-faced child eating pain au chocolat.

Luke was there trailing behind me in the street while I arched my back to capture the perfect picture of a gargoyle scowling down at me from a roof, smiling behind his sunglasses when I bumped lightly into an old woman carrying her groceries back from the market. He seemed perfectly at home in Paris, a vision of masculine charm in his tight sky blue button-down shirt and navy slacks. He turned heads, and people smiled at us when we put our arms around each other and peered into shop windows, or laughed about some private joke. I couldn't help but stop what I was doing every once in a while to walk over to him and steal a kiss, or a sip of the espresso drink in his to-go cup.

"I still can't believe we're here," I said as we strolled hand in hand along the Seine. Leaves that had drifted on the wind floated along beside us at a lazy pace. "I can't believe you brought me."

"You deserve it," Luke said. "I didn't want you to have to wait until next summer to see Paris, and I didn't want you to have to spend your whole time in France working your ass off at some summer study program."

I leaned my head against his shoulder as we walked, the weight of my camera in its bag secure against my hip. I pulled my hair up on top of my head in a swirling bun, and passersby could probably see the little purple love bite he had bruised into my neck that morning, but I didn't care. I was in love, and I was in Paris, and that was all that mattered.

Luke and I had been officially dating for a few months, which had led to a media frenzy, but it died down soon enough. I changed my publicly listed email to stop reporters begging for an interview, and I got used to seeing the occasional candid photo of Luke and me out to dinner in the local papers. We changed my job title at work so that I was no longer technically working in Luke's department, clearing up any possible accusations of abuse of power on his end, and I had quietly finished my internship without any pushback from school authorities. Luke spoke very highly and very defensively of me at a couple of press events, asking that our privacy please be respected. Strangely, we had reached a new equilibrium as things settled, and now being the infamous Luke Thorpe's girlfriend felt as natural to me as breathing.

"You must be excited to come back here next summer for your program," he said. "Everything will be in full bloom then."

"Actually.... I've been thinking about that." I pulled away a bit and looked up into his face. He took his sunglasses off and slid them into his breast pocket so I could see his eyes. He was concerned.

"What is it?"

"I've just been thinking... What if I didn't come back to France?"

"Emily what do you mean? I thought you were enjoying yourself."

"I am enjoying myself! This is the most amazing trip of my life. I'm stupidly, blissfully happy but... I'm happiest because you're here, Luke. And I've seen Paris now, with you, without anyone breathing down my neck trying to get me to go to class or an internship. I couldn't imagine choosing to do that now."

Luke squeezed my arm.

"So you'll be staying in New York next summer?"

"I think so. I'd like to, anyway. I like... I like spending my time with you."

"Aw, baby," Luke said, tipping my chin up with his fingers and giving me a sweet kiss. "I don't want to keep you from traveling."

"You're not; I promise. I want to be with you, Luke. I want to help you with the charity and spend more time with your family. I want you to meet my family, too, if you'd like to."

My heart was racing in my chest. We had been an official couple for some time now, spending the nights at each other's house and making time for regular dates, but this seemed like a new, bigger step. This was me admitting that I wanted our lives together to continue into the next year, to become increasingly entwined, and that I wanted to become an integral part of his life.

Luke's green eyes searched my face and then he smiled, pulling me in for a deep kiss. We were blocking foot traffic on the path, but people just weaved around us. I would never get over how easily I melted into him, how quickly the rest of the world fell away. When he looked at me, I felt like I was the only woman in the world. Certainly, the only one that mattered.

When he pulled away from me, his eyes were glowing with delight.

"I'd absolutely like that."

I beamed and opened my mouth to reply, but I was cut off by the tinny ringing of Luke's cellphone. He took the call and answered it as we strolled along the path, his arm around my shoulder, my arm around his waist.

"Olivia? How is everything over there?"

I was proud of Luke for actually stepping away from work for a week to come to Paris with me. The trip had been his idea, a surprise gift for finishing up my internship with SkyBlue. He had left Olivia and Carl in charge as co-parents of his baby and had been checking his phone for text updates from both of them for the entire trip. To his credit, he had done his very best to not check during meals or when we were in bed together, but I could tell it was hard for him. I found his workaholic tendencies as amusing as they were admirable, but it meant the world to me that he was making such an effort to be present with me.

"What do you mean?" He asked now, slowing his pace. "Well if you've got something you want to tell me, just come on out and say it. You're making me nervous, Olivia."

There was a long pause as he listened, eyebrows drawn together tightly. I lingered near one of the stone walls overlooking the river, doing my best to at least look like I wasn't eavesdropping. Luke didn't seem to mind when I was around when he took his calls, but I had gotten into the habit of not involving myself too closely when I was still his employee, just to protect his privacy. Because Luke had his hands in so much of the inner workings of his company, you never knew what kind of call he was going to take. It could be about a hiring or a firing, or a big investment decision, or in-house gossip about SkyBlue stocks. But now, it was hard not to listen. Had something gone wrong? Had Carl buckled under the pressure like Sonia bet me he would and choked during a press meeting, or a R&D session?

Luke stared at the cobblestones hard, saying nothing for a long while. Then he took a deep breath.

"You're kidding. You have got to be kidding."

I strained to hear Olivia's response, but the phone speakers were muffled by the ambient noise around us. I twined my fingers in and out of each other in a lattice, wondering if I was allowed to ask about what was going on, or if I should? After all, I didn't work for Luke anymore, or SkyBlue. I was sure there was something to be said for not involving significant others too deeply in the affairs of a huge, highly valued company. And I wasn't particularly interested in getting embroiled in the sort of stress and drama that tended to keep Luke up at night. I had woken up enough times to find him listless and awake, or sitting on the edge of the bed answering emails on his phone. I could usually entice him back to sleep by putting my arms around him and asking nicely, but there was no amount of money or power in the world that could persuade me to take on his workload. Not in a million years.

"No, no, I understand..." Luke said, pacing a tight circle there on the sidewalk. A mother with a stroller dodged to avoid him. "Listen this is definitely something we need to talk about when I get back but for right now... Just don't burn the place down alright? Thank you for telling me."

Luke put his phone away with a stunned expression. I don't

think I had ever seen him look so shocked, not even when the paparazzi had caught us kissing behind the hotel in San Francisco. He wasn't angry, per se, or distressed. Just absolutely taken aback.

"What is it?" I asked. For all my deliberation, I wanted to know. I always wanted to see inside his ever-whirring mind, to know what was eating at him or exciting him, "What's wrong?"

"Nothing's wrong," He said with a disbelieving laugh. There was a strange gleam in his eyes. "But things just got a lot messier over in the States."

"Messy how?"

"Remember when I told you if anything ever happened to Olivia, SkyBlue would fold like a house of cards?"

"Oh God, is she okay?"

"She's fine. Better than fine. But, well... Olivia's been hooking up with some new guy and you'll never guess who."

I blinked in surprise. How could that possible affect her work life, or be messy for SkyBlue? If anything, getting out more and seeing someone would do wonders for her disposition. I wasn't sure I wanted to know the answer, but I asked anyway.

"Who?"

Luke smirked to himself as he put his sunglasses back on, shaking his head.

"Carl. My CFO."

AFTERWORD

Thank You for reading "Beauty and the BOSS".

Have you read the FREE Prequel yet? If not, you can download this at below link

[Click HERE to Download the FREE Prequel](#)

I also have an Exclusive Reader Group where I post latest Release and Free promotion updates. Click the link below if you would like to be a part of this fun loving group!

Join R.S. Elliot's Exclusive Reader Group

SNEEK-PEEK INTO BOOK 2 OF THE BILLIONAIRE'S OBSESSION SERIES

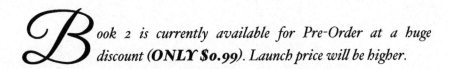

*ook 2 is currently available for Pre-Order at a huge discount (**ONLY $0.99**). Launch price will be higher.*

Click HERE to Pre-Order Book 2 NOW!

CHAPTER 2

I walked to the very edge of campus at the end of the school day, a thin veil of sweat breaking out on my forehead despite the cool weather. Something could go wrong at any second; someone could see me and get suspicious, or a teacher could come over and ask what I was doing walking the perimeter of the school. But no one said anything, and the distant shouts and laughter of kids waiting for the bus in messy clumps didn't draw any nearer.

Right on time, Aiden pulled up in his Sedan, smirking at me behind his sunglasses.

"Your carriage awaits, my lady," he said, unlocking the passenger side door.

"Very suave," I replied, and tucked myself away in the car as fast as I could. Then, before I knew it, we were careening down the road together, Aiden's stereo blasting our song, a huge grin of relief spreading across my face. We had really done it. Snuck off together without anyone being the wiser. The feeling of success was totally intoxicating, like the glass of sparkling wine I had been handed by a freewheeling aunt at last year's family Christmas dinner. I felt totally weightless, totally alive and full of light.

Is this what freedom felt like?

"Oh my God, I can't believe we're doing this!" I said with a laugh, wind blowing through the rolled-down windows and whipping my hair around my face.

"Are you happy?" Aiden asked with a sidelong smirk at me. He was pushing the speed limit, taking curves hard and tight to illicit delighted giggles from me.

"So happy. You have no idea."

"I bet it feels pretty good to not have your dad breathing down your neck, huh? I don't think we've ever really been able to have an entire evening to ourselves. You always got picked up early or my parents called me home or we were out in public with other people around to bother us."

"This is so much nicer," I agreed heartily, kicking up the stereo a bit more. Aiden's house was in the opposite direction from mine but it wasn't very far away from the school, but he was taking the winding backroads to make our ride last a little longer. This was one of his favorite tricks to eke out just a little more time with me, and he had used it often when we were still just awkwardly talking to each other about school and algebra. We would circle blocks and zip through old backroads, letting the radio fill the heavy silence between us or talking until our tongues were tired. The first time he kissed me, it had been on one of those needlessly long drives home.

Now he gave me one of his irresistible smiles, the ones that showed up on the sports page of our local newspaper whenever our team, the Hawks, won a game.

"Good," Aiden said. "It's about to get even better."

"Oh yeah?"

'I've got dinner planned for us. Like, a real cook-it-in-the-kitchen dinner. You like Italian, right?"

"I love it! Are you serious?"

"Yup. I went grocery shopping this morning and everything. I figured if I have you around I might as well show off a little bit. My mom's been teaching me how to cook, and you know she's a wizard in the kitchen."

"I'd love that," I said, reaching for the free hand that rested on his knee. We interlaced our fingers together and I leaned back and closed my eyes, enjoying the rumble of the car beneath me and the cool breezes across my face. I never wanted to forget what this sort of perfect happiness felt like, so I diligently committed every detail of it to memory.

Aiden and his parents lived in a simple A-frame house painted bright blue. It was situated at the end of a tucked away cul de sac lined with trees that cast long trails of shade, and to my knowledge, Aiden had lived in that cul de sac all his life. We were both only children, although Aiden's parents still lived together whereas mine had gotten divorced when I was five. He had grown up with a creek trickling through his backyard and a tire swing hung from the big oak out front. It seemed like an ideal sort of childhood, and he always talked about it with fondness.

"Here we are," he said, putting the car into park. "Home sweet home."

"And your parents aren't around?"

"Nope, they cleared off this morning. They'll be back Sunday night. We've got free run of the place."

I had been inside of Aiden's house plenty of times before.

His parents seemed to genuinely like me and were always inviting me in for cookies and a chat, or over for dinner some nights to catch up with the both of us. But this felt entirely different. When I walked in the door, I wasn't greeted by his father sitting in his usual chair with the newspaper, or by his mother, calling out my name from the kitchen while she whipped something for us. The house was perfectly, blessedly quiet, and I was very aware that we were the only ones in it. We could have been entering into our first apartment together for the first time and it would have felt the same.

"Want me to get dinner started?" Aiden asked, tossing down his backpack on the couch and moving past me into the kitchen.

"Yeah, that would be great."

Aiden hadn't been lying. His mother had taught him some pretty neat tricks. I watched on in delight as he simmered garlic and basil for homemade marinara sauce, and helped him measure out oil and spices for the stuffed ravioli. Soon the kitchen was full of the heady scent of oregano and thyme, and in no time at all Aiden was plating up big steaming servings of pasta and sauce. When I took my first bite, I thought I had been transported to heaven.

"This is amazing!"

"It's not as good as my mom's," Aiden said, sinking down into the big comfy couch in the family den. This was usually where we sat with his parents, or studied together while his mother chaperoned from the kitchen. "But it's pretty tasty!"

I got us both tall glasses of ice water and soon we were enjoying our dinner together, nestled close on the couch. Everything about it felt so effortless and natural, and even though I knew I was getting ahead of myself, I couldn't help but think that this is what our evenings together could be like in the future, if we got married and got a place together. We would be able to meet each other after work and cook, then eat together in the privacy of our own home like real adults and talk about how our days had gone. There would be no one to tell us what to do and what not to do, just us, and our love for each other. I couldn't help but smile at the thought.

"What's going on in that pretty head?" Aiden asked. He swiped a bit of marinara sauce off my cheek with his thumb and then sucked his thumb off in his mouth. The gesture was probably thoughtless for him, but there was something indescribably sexy about it that sent a wave of heat through my body.

"Nothing," I said shyly. "I'm just happy."

"Just how I like you."

He leaned over to kiss my nose, making me giggle. We ate the rest of our dinner in happy conversation, talking about movies, our classmates, our teachers, anything but schoolwork. I never wanted to step out of this moment, to stop sitting on this couch with the guy I was in love with, eating a delicious dinner and discussing our lives. But I have always been responsible, even on days when I was supposed to be cutting loose a little bit.

"Well," I said, pushing my empty bowl of pasta away from me on the coffee table. "Do you think we ought to get to studying?"

Aiden made a face.

"Ugh, right. Studying."

"The sooner we get it done the sooner we can do something else," I offered.

Aiden nodded as he stood and began to clear away our plates.

"You're right. Let me rinse these off and I'll grab the books. I'll warn you, I've only gotten worse since we studied together in algebra class."

"I'll be the judge of that."

As much as I wanted to be optimistic about the whole matter, Aiden was right. He had gotten worse, or at least not gotten any better. School wasn't his strong suit but math was his worst subject by far and we both knew it. I suspected he might have a touch of dyslexia that made keeping numbers straight hard, or he was just terrible at the foundations of high school level math, and that made everything that came after harder. It wasn't that Aiden was stupid. He was sharp as a whip when it came to playing football, cooking, building things in shop class, fixing cards, or taking care of kids. Anything he could do with his hands, and learn by doing until he got it right, he was great at. But asking him to learn something from reading instructions out of a book was virtually guaranteed to bring about failure.

Still, I tried. I pulled out the scrap paper and drew him diagrams, tilting them this way and that so he could see them from different angles. We tried to talk through his assignments, with my scribbling down notes for him to reference later. I even tried to teach him new ways of solving the equations, running through every tip and trick I had learned during my time in the class. Nothing seemed to help, even though Aiden tried his best. I kept up a positive exterior, but inside, I was nervous. Aiden had to pass this class or he would be held back, and that would derail his graduation schedule.

"I don't think we're getting anywhere," he said with a sigh. He tossed down his pencil and pressed the heels of his hands to his eyes. A glance at the clock told me that we had been at this almost an hour, and we had only managed to successfully navigate three of the questions on his assignment.

"You're doing alright," I urged in a soothing voice. "It's all about exponential growth. Eventually some part of this will click, and then another and another."

"If you say so." Aiden rotated one of his shoulders and winced.

"Still hurting from practice?"

"Nothing serious. I should probably ice it, or take a hot shower."

"Why don't you shower?" I offered. "It might be good to take a step back from all this and unwind."

"You're sure you're alright out here by yourself."

"Yes," I said with a laugh, urging him on towards the hallway towards the rest of the house. "I'll find some way to entertain myself."

Aiden leaned down to give me one more kiss, then disappeared down the hallway to soak his arching shoulders. Dating an athlete, you got used to the cramps and pains. I was amazed that he was in one piece at all after the abuse he took on the field.

I scrubbed the dishes left in the sink while Aiden showered, taking care to line them up neatly to dry. It was the least I could do after the amazing meal he had made for us. Once again, my mind wandered to the future. Is this what it would be like for us? Evenings at home doing little domestic things like chores and treating sports injuries. Things like that had never seemed exciting to me before, certainly not when my parents were forced to live together and function as a unit while fighting each other at every turn. But this was easy. Fun, even.

"Mia?" Aiden called from down the hall. He must have cracked the door to the bathroom, because i could hear the shower running in the distance. "Could you come here a sec?"

"Sure!" I replied.

I walked down the hallway towards the bathroom following the sound of the shower and the plume of steam in the hall. The door had been left cracked, and I gently pushed it open a few more inches. Aiden was standing in front of the mirror with a towel wrapped around his waist, his chest gleaming from the shower while water dripped from his hair. He was rotating his shoulder, looking at it in the mirror, and barely glanced over his shoulder at me.

"Would you get me the arnica salve? It's in my bedroom, I think."

"Sure," I said, my voice coming out strangely hoarse. My face was hot.

I ducked back into the hallway and pushed my way into his room, snatching up the tube of arnica cream from on top of his dresser. The room smelled like him, like worn linens and his favorite wool sweaters and the cheap mall cologne he spritzed on when we went out for dinner dates. Somehow, this only made the heat in my face grow worse, and I realized my mouth had gone dry.

Aiden turned to take the medicine from me, stepping close as he did so, and I found myself enveloped in the humid warmth of the little room and in the sight of him, barely dressed. I had seen him strip off his shirt on the field before but this was a whole lot more skin, a whole lot more intimate. I wondered if he cared that I was seeing him like this, or if part of him had called me out here so I could.

My skin was on fire, screaming out for his touch. My lips burned when his hot breath passed over them, and I shuddered as he slid his strong hands around my waist. I felt powerless and powerful at the same time, pulled tight as a violin string by the push and pull of our desires. I thought for sure if something didn't resolve soon I would snap from the tension. Aiden took the bottle from my hands. Then he discarded it on the bathroom counter, took my face in his hands, and pulled me into an all-consuming kiss.

I had felt desire when I was around Aiden before, and I was familiar with the wave of throbbing heat that overtook me when he kissed me between classes or wrapped me up in his arms after games when he was hot and triumphant and wearing a grin so wide it could have stunned me at twenty paces. I had trembled under his touch when I let him fondle my breasts in the back of his car for a few minutes before I had scrambled out of the car, overheated and overwhelmed by the feelings building inside me. Aiden had been patient with how skittish I got about intimacy, and we had never had sex before, never been this close with so few clothes between us.

This realization made me a little dizzy, but I didn't pull away. My usual fear had melted away into something stronger, a burning want that gave me a sense of sureness I hadn't known before. I had of course thought about giving it up to Aiden. I had deliberated about it and daydreamed about it and fantasized about it some nights, with my fingers between my legs under the sheets and my free hand clamped over my mouth to keep from squealing. I knew I wanted it to be him, that I wanted to feel his muscled body moving on top of mine while he looked into my eyes and told me that he loved me. No matter what happened after tonight, I knew what I wanted.

I deepened the kiss, spreading my eager fingers across Aiden's broad chest. His skin was warm and still wet from the shower, and the chill drops of water dripping from his hair onto my collarbone made me shiver with delight. His hand came up under my chin, gently tipping my face up so he could more easily slip his tongue into my mouth, and the next thing I knew I was being walked backwards into his bedroom.

I climbed onto his bed eagerly, pulling him behind me until we were both kneeling on the comforter, arms locked around each other, kissing intently.

"Mia," Aiden said, his words a hot smear against my mouth as I kissed him insistently, not even wanting him to stop to say a word. "Baby, I-"

"Yes?"

"I don't want to do this unless you're sure."

I nuzzled my nose against him, chasing his mouth for another few needy kisses before taking a moment to catch my breath. I looked into his eyes, a brown so deep I could fall into them and never find myself again. They were full of love and lust, desire and concern. I had never wanted him more than I did in that moment.

"I'm sure. I want this."

〜

*Book 2 is currently available for Pre-Order at a huge discount (**ONLY $0.99**). Launch price will be higher.*

Click HERE to Pre-Order Book 2 NOW!

Made in the USA
Middletown, DE
28 December 2020

30317886R00136